WHO DARES?

*For my husband, Douglas Bell, with love and
thanks for always daring to believe in me
and for countless family holidays in Lorne*

First American Edition 2011
Kane Miller, A Division of EDC Publishing

Copyright © Krista Bell 2005
First published 2005
www.kristabell.com

Cover design by Courtney Dom
Illustrations by Damien Bell
Text design by Paulene Meyer

Library of Congress Control Number:2010942741
Printed and bound in the United States of America
1 2 3 4 5 6 7 8 9 10
ISBN: 978-1-61067-047-0

WHO DARES?

Krista Blakeney Bell

Kane Miller

A DIVISION OF EDC PUBLISHING

One

"Look at me! Look at me!" Rhys was fooling around on the second-floor balcony of the posh resort, but as he climbed up onto the raised planter he slipped. Falling forward, he lunged awkwardly at the metal railing and stopped himself.

"Whoa, take it easy!" Toby grabbed at Rhys's arm and pulled him back. "We've only just got here.

Try not to kill yourself in the first two minutes! Dad reckons you're so focused on surfing that you're sure to win the Juniors – but hey, you won't have a chance at the surfing title if you fall off the building. Anyway, if you wanted to go BASE jumping, you should've said so – and we could have brought a parachute." Toby elbowed him to emphasize the joke.

"You kidding?" Rhys steadied himself. "I'm here to surf. How good are those waves? This is awesome. And check out the new skate park." He pointed along the beach in the gloomy twilight to show Toby what he was talking about.

"I've stayed in Lorne since I was a kid, but never this close to the water. The grandparents' house is OK – except you know how far up the hill it is. But this, this is insane – it's almost on the beach. A whole week at the Cumberland – this is so cool. Your parents are brilliant, Toby. Thanks for bringing me."

"Get real! We wouldn't have come here if you hadn't been so keen and signed us all up." Toby lightly punched his friend's arm. "You're the one who wanted to be here for the comp. You're the one who put our names down – *and* you're the one who hasn't stopped talking about it since. We could hardly come without you, could we? Besides, there's the dare. You made me a promise – and I'm going to hold you to it!"

Rhys didn't reply. He was mesmerized by the roar of the surf. Watching the huge waves crashing onto the sand, he reluctantly recalled his last trip to Lorne, just months before. It had been Toby's first visit, and in lots of ways it had been a total disaster – but, then again, if they hadn't stayed together at Rhys grandparents' place last summer, they would never have become friends.

And Rhys's mum would never have gotten the help she needed with her addiction – she was definitely getting better each week, although Rhys knew she still had a long way to go. It had been tough confronting his mother's illness, but he was here to surf, so he desperately tried to push away the memories that threatened to overwhelm him.

"This setup is great!" Rhys sighed. The horror

of his mother's accident and its repercussions were still so fresh in his memory.

Toby had found out the truth: Rhys's mother wasn't just weird – she was sick, really sick, but she had finally accepted professional help and gone to a clinic. With the help of Toby and his parents, things had already improved for the whole Morton family. Rhys's dad was more like the dad he remembered – and his big brother was living at home again. Things were much better.

Wanting to move on now, Rhys searched for something else to talk about. "Did I tell you this is the first time I've come to Lorne without Mum or Dad or my brother?" It was lame, but all he could manage.

"Only …" Toby feigned counting on his fingers "… a few hundred times." He laughed. "Anyway, I'm starving. Let's check out what we're doing for dinner. We could grab some Chinese like last time. That fried rice is great. But the fish and chips downstairs are the best. Hmmm. Let's see what Mum and Dad want."

As Rhys followed Toby back into the living

room of the suite, they caught the end of a telephone conversation that Toby's dad was having.

"We'll see you downstairs in fifteen minutes, Edmund. Yes, I made a reservation. Looking forward to meeting your family. Cheers." Mr. Hampshire hung up the phone.

"What's going on, Dad?" asked Toby. "We're starving."

"That's lucky." Mr. Hampshire smiled at his wife, and then looked back at the boys. "We've got a dinner date downstairs at Aqua. One of the partners from work is here with his family, too. They've got a boy about your age. I thought it'd be nice for you guys to 'hook up' – is that the right expression?"

"Something like that." Toby made a face at Rhys, rolling his eyes. Rhys shared his friend's disappointment. Unlike last vacation, Toby and Rhys were actually looking forward to spending time together just hanging out, enjoying each other's company. "Whatever. Give us ten." Toby smiled at his father and then headed down the hallway towards the bedrooms.

Rhys followed Toby to the room they'd be sharing for the next week, to sort out his gear and get changed for dinner. He dumped the stuff from his backpack onto the floor. With any luck this other boy would have friends of his own and have no interest in hanging out with Rhys and Toby.

TWO

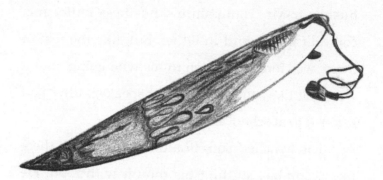

"The Champagne cocktails were out of this world."
Mrs. Lynch had such an annoying voice. She was
holding the dinner table captive with her boring
story about some cocktail party she'd been to,
oblivious to the effect she was having on the others
at the table. "It's such a pity you missed it. Everyone
was there, weren't they, Edmund?"

She didn't even glance at her husband when she spoke to him, but continued talking so stridently that Rhys was embarrassed for Toby's parents. They were eating their meals and politely pretending to be interested in the one-sided conversation. Her husband, Mr. Hampshire's business colleague, couldn't get a word in either, but, like the rest of them, was forced to listen to his wife going on – it was a bit like some of the guest speakers Rhys had listened to at school assemblies.

The Lynches' son, Braddon, was sitting there like a zombie, stuffing his mouth with food. He was totally ignoring everybody, including Toby and Rhys, who were sitting on either side of him.

It wasn't as though the boys hadn't tried to get Braddon to talk to them – they had, but with no success. When the Lynches had finally arrived at the restaurant twenty minutes late, Braddon had plonked himself down in the chair at the far end of the table. He hadn't even acknowledged they were there.

All they'd managed to get out of him since

was what he wanted for dinner – which included a plate of chips that he had refused to share. Rhys didn't need to talk to Toby about him – he knew that there was no way they'd be spoiling their vacation hanging out with this loser. No way.

"It was *the* bon voyage party of the century, wasn't it, Edmund?" Mrs. Lynch droned on, hardly pausing to breathe. "It was at Shiloh's *gorgeous* chateau – well, it's not really a chateau, of course, but it certainly felt like one that night. We were all out on the flagstone patio and the olive trees were strung with twinkling lights. We were looking out at the shimmering ocean at sunset, while we sipped Bollinger Champagne and ate pheasant pâté, barbecued shrimp and freshly-shucked oysters. I could almost believe I was summering in France."

Rhys wondered how much longer this would go on. He wanted to talk to Toby, but Mrs. Lynch's piercing voice made that impossible.

She stopped to have a couple of sips of her Champagne. Rhys shuddered – he couldn't help it. He wished she *were* in France so he hadn't met her.

There was something about her – something familiar that made Rhys feel uncomfortable. But even though he'd only known them for an hour, and didn't like Mrs. Lynch or her son, Rhys hoped she didn't have the same problem as his mum. He wouldn't wish that on any family – even the Lynches.

"The whole effect was delightful." Mrs. Lynch just didn't seem to know when to stop. "Everyone was wearing such gorgeous outfits – I was most impressed. It really was like being in Paris! And did I tell you that Shiloh's latest sculpture is being exhibited here at the Qudos Gallery while she's away? The sale of that one piece will pay for her trip to Europe! Amazing, isn't it?" She frowned for a moment, but immediately resumed talking. "Goodness, I've just realized – I hope she's got security and a decent insurance policy – her house is full of such treasures – and no one's staying there while she's gone. But we're such good friends, we'll just keep an eye on things for her while we're here, won't we, Edmund? Nothing's too much trouble for dear Shiloh."

Rhys pushed the last of his food around his plate and groaned silently. He noticed that Mrs. Lynch had a few more mouthfuls of her Champagne, but, before anyone else had the chance to speak, she was at it again. On and on and on. How much longer? Rhys wondered. Someone interrupt her. Please.

"Shiloh's such a talented artist – a living legend. We're so lucky – we got to know her years ago, before she was famous, when we bought our beach house up on the ridge; it's just along the path from hers, you know. You must come for drinks one evening this week. We'll make a date before we leave tonight, shall we? It'll be so much fun for Braddon. The boys can have a sleepover that night. Now that's a nice idea, isn't it? Good, that's settled then."

Rhys shuddered again. No, it's not. He hoped Mrs. Hampshire wouldn't accept the invitation without asking them first because he knew that a sleepover at Braddon Lynch's house was the last thing he and Toby were interested in doing. No, definitely not. How old did she think they were, anyway? They were fourteen, not four. She was so out of touch and so bossy that, for a split second, Rhys actually felt sorry for Braddon.

Finally Mrs. Lynch stopped blabbering on long enough to have a mouthful of the food that was starting to congeal on her plate.

"So, Toby." Mr. Lynch coughed and looked embarrassed as he grabbed the unexpected opportunity to speak. "Your dad mentioned that you and Rhys are entering the Easter Surf Competition. That's exciting. Why don't you tell us what's involved? I know Braddon would be really interested. He's always wanted to learn to surf, haven't you, Braddon?"

But before Toby had a chance to respond to the question, Braddon had pushed back his chair and bolted from the table. Rhys was stunned. Braddon had totally ignored his father, and just like his mother, hadn't even made eye contact with him. Rhys guessed he was heading for the bathroom, but it was a bit odd. And very rude. Rhys's dad would have gone after him and made him apologize, if Rhys had been stupid enough to do that sort of thing.

From Rhys's viewpoint, it wasn't Mr. Lynch who was embarrassing – it was Braddon's mother who'd had everybody squirming. Rhys raised his eyebrows at Toby – and Toby responded by shrugging his shoulders. What was this guy's problem?

Three

"Look, I know you're not sure about the comp, Tobes, but it'll be fun." Rhys and Toby were crossing Mountjoy Parade in front of the resort, their surfboards under their arms.

It was the morning after the dreadful dinner with the Lynches – at least they wouldn't bump into any of those weirdos in the water. The Easter Surf

Competition started in a couple of days, so, having checked the surf from the balcony of the resort, Rhys had suggested that he and Toby go down to the beach for a morning practice session. The waves looked perfect.

It was months since either of them had been in the surf. Rhys knew that because Toby had only learned to surf last vacation, he needed to spend as much time as he could before the competition practicing on his new surfboard. Since Toby hadn't done much surfing, Rhys had entered him in the Junior Novice section. Rhys knew his friend was only going in it because Rhys had pestered him until he'd said yes – and because he'd dared him, and they had a bet riding on it.

Rhys had only made that dumb bet so that Toby would agree to compete, and because of it, Rhys now sort of hoped that Toby didn't do too well – Rhys didn't want to lose the bet! But at the same time it'd be good if Toby got at least third – just so long as he didn't win, or come second. Yeah, third would be good, and then Rhys would be off the hook – and

Toby would be very pleased with himself. Sounded like a plan.

"I reckon you'll do OK on your new board." Rhys was really impressed. "Your dad is so cool. First he goes shopping and then he buys you this. It's perfect. My dad wouldn't have known what shop to go into, let alone what board to buy. I wish my dad knew something about surfing. Your dad's awesome. So is he going to use your board in the Easter Surf?"

"Maybe, but I think he'd like to use your Quiksilver, if that's OK." Toby sounded tentative. Rhys wondered when Toby would realize that he'd do whatever he could in an attempt to repay the Hampshires for their help in getting his mother's life back on track.

"Of course your dad can borrow my board." Rhys shook his head and grinned. "It's the right size for him – he'll have even more chance of winning if he uses this one. And it's still pretty new, too. I haven't used it much since I got it from the grandparents for my last birthday. Hey, how cool would it be if my board wins two events: Juniors and Geriatrics?"

They shared the joke, but Rhys knew that was a definite possibility. Mr. Hampshire had been a surfing champion when he was young – no reason he couldn't do it again in the Veterans.

As they walked down the steps towards the surf club, Rhys suddenly realized that he'd been feeling uneasy since he'd met that awful woman the night before. He needed to talk about it.

"Mrs. Lynch tries too hard, doesn't she?" Rhys hoped that had sounded casual. "It's like she's got something to prove. I don't know, but there's something about her, isn't there?" It was ridiculous, but he felt kind of spooked, and he needed some sort of reassurance about Braddon's mother. Meeting her here in Lorne had brought back too many nightmarish memories.

"She kinda reminds me of my mum." Rhys stumbled on – it was difficult to admit, but it was true. "You know, she hides things by being all gushy and over the top. Remember how Mum carried on when she first met you? Well, I reckon Mrs. Lynch is a bit like that. You don't think she's …" Rhys struggled to say it out loud. "You don't think she's like my mum, do you? You don't think she's sick, too, do you? It's just she talks so much about nothing – and I don't know … what do you think?"

"I don't know either, but I do know you're paranoid." Toby laughed and slapped Rhys on the back. "You're overreacting. You think everyone's got some major secret. But maybe she's just one of those housewives who stays home with nothing much to do. You know, she's only got one kid. They live in Toorak. She probably goes shopping and out to lunch every day because she can. She might just be bored."

Toby lifted his surfboard onto his head. "Sometimes my mum jokes about wanting to stay home and do nothing but shop," he confided, "but then she says it would be so boring not having a career. I reckon the Lynches have lots of money – and Mr. Lynch seems heaps older than his wife. Maybe he doesn't want her to work – my granddad was like that about my grandma. Anyway, who cares?

It's their problem, not yours. Forget about it. Look at that surf!"

And then Toby was striding down the beach in front of the surf club, looking as though he was going to dive straight into the water. He had thrown his board bag onto the sand next to the stone wall, but he was having trouble zipping up his wetsuit while he tried to balance his surfboard on his hip with the other hand. He looked so comical hopping around in a circle that Rhys grinned and tried to push away the haunting image of Mrs. Lynch.

And then Rhys realized that he was being totally stupid – Toby was right – he was worrying about something that had nothing to do with him. He didn't know Mrs. Lynch – he didn't even like her. She had just triggered bad memories and Rhys had overreacted. With any luck, he'd never see her again. End of story.

As he watched Toby continue to struggle with his board and wetsuit, Rhys laughed out loud. Toby finally dropped his board in frustration and twisted around to reach his zip cord, falling onto the sand in the process.

"Hey, Surfer Joe, chill." Rhys was really enjoying Toby's uncoordinated attempt to rush into the surf. He smiled at Toby, whose face and hair were now coated in sand, and rested one foot on top of his back, as if to hold him down. "There's no rush, dude." Rhys obviously needed to remind Toby that they had a routine to follow. "There's a couple of things to do before you hit the surf, remember? First we wax the boards. It's months since mine was in the water – and yours is brand new, so you need to do it properly. I'll help – you've got to get it right or you'll have real hassles standing up. Then we're going to do a warm-up run."

Without hesitating, Toby sprang onto both feet as if he was already riding the board, then he ran up the beach and retrieved the new block of wax from his board bag. For the next few minutes, with the sound of the breaking waves behind them, they waxed their surfboards until Rhys was sure both boards were perfect.

Rhys was curious as to why Toby had been in

such a hurry to get into the water. It seemed a bit weird, almost as though Toby were running away from something, rather than to it. It was strange because Rhys knew Toby wasn't afraid of the waves anymore, although he had been when he first learned to surf.

Since then, Rhys had taught Toby how to handle the surf – to be confident and work with the waves, not fight against them. So, if he wasn't scared of the water, there must be something else that was making him so quiet all of a sudden.

"You OK with this, Tobes?" Rhys tried to sound casual as they did their warm-up run, down to the breakwater and back.

"Yeah." Toby sounded a bit hesitant. "No. It sort of feels like riding a surfboard is something I did in a dream – not for real. I kind of know I did surf here a couple of months ago, but I still don't really believe it. Yeah, I'm OK."

"So what's with the frown?"

Rhys had to build up his friend's confidence so they could enjoy their week together in the surf –

and do well in the competition. Until last vacation, Rhys had always surfed alone, but once Toby had started riding a board, it had been much more fun sharing the surf with a friend.

"Don't sweat it, Toby. You'll be fine. Remember you were taught by the expert, soon-to-be Junior Surf Champion of Lorne – Rhys Alexander Morton," he boomed, in a mock announcer's voice.

Rhys figured it'd be best to get Toby into the surf before he had more time to think about things. So he put his arms into the long sleeves of his wetsuit and pulled the cord behind his waist to zip it up. He knew that the water would be pretty cold. "OK, dude? Who dares?" he shouted over his shoulder, casually checking that his friend was following him down the beach.

He watched as Toby flung his wax at his board bag and took off towards the water with his new board under his arm, looking like a seasoned surfer.

"I'm with you!" Toby yelled, as he caught up at the water's edge.

Four

Rhys and Toby crashed through the surf in unison. They paddled out the back to wait for the right wave in what were now regular, well-formed sets. The water was icy on Rhys's face. This was what he missed so much in the city – it was invigorating.

"Paradise! I love this." He spat out a mouthful of salty water. "Who'd be anywhere else? Not me.

Here comes a beauty, Toby. Paddle hard. Let's go. That's it. Paddle. Paddle. Yes!"

And then they were both lifted up by a perfectly formed, blue-green, crystal clear wave that thrust them forward like a wild ride at a theme park.

"Quick," Rhys shouted, over the roar of the breaking wave. "Stand up. Now!"

But, as Rhys got to his feet, he saw Toby slip and crash down onto his board. He managed to hang on and ride it prone, like a bodyboard. Never mind, he'd pick it up again soon enough! Rhys knew Toby would be OK – he was a quick learner and he had strong legs because he was a tap dancer.

Now Rhys had to concentrate on his own ride. He moved expertly up and down his board, enjoying the ride, crisscrossing back and forth along the face of the wave, ducking in and out of the curl, making it work for him. Spray covered his face, and he threw back his head with satisfaction, flicking the wet strands of hair out of his eyes.

Rhys rode that wave like the champion he hoped to become this week, right here, where he'd been surfing all his life. He pumped it all the way along the beach, until he expertly flicked off the back of the wave. Totally satisfied, he watched as it dissolved into nothingness right next to the rocks. Brilliant, totally, utterly brilliant.

Nothing, but nothing, was better than surfing! It was what had helped him stay sane over the last few years, while he'd been coping with his mother's illness. Surfing had been something to focus on – it had given his life some purpose. And this new board was awesome, although admittedly he was still getting to know its capabilities – and, each time he took it out, he found he could push it harder and it would respond.

Until recently Rhys had never believed in himself enough to enter the Easter Surf, but because things had changed so much for his family in the last few months, he now had the courage to give it a try. And he knew his friendship with Toby was an important part of his newfound confidence.

"Now *that* was a wave!" Rhys paddled out to where Toby was waiting for him. "You'll nail it next time, dude. But how did that feel?"

"I'd forgotten how awesome it is." Toby was grinning like some silly cartoon cat. "It's so different from the high I get when I dance. I mean, tapping in a comp always gives me a huge rush – but not like this. This is way different. When I tap I'm in complete control, but this is like me versus the surf. It was excellent, but I need to practice heaps. Let's go again."

"Cool." Rhys was pleased – this week would be the best vacation ever. "You'll do it next time for sure. You can choose the wave."

And so they waited out the back for the best wave in the next set, with Toby managing to stay up for at least part of the way.

Several hours zipped past as they rode wave after exhilarating wave, with Rhys yelling advice to Toby while experimenting with some new tricks himself, working towards producing his best form on competition day. The board performed to his expectations, and more – it was incredible.

"We should go in for lunch. What do you

reckon?" Rhys asked Toby finally, as they lay on their boards and bobbed in the swell. "The waves have dropped off anyway."

"Yeah, I could do with a break." Toby stood up in the shallow water and undid his ankle strap. "I'm wrecked."

As they walked up the beach, Rhys was surprised to see the time on the surf club clock. "Whoa, we were out there much longer than I thought." Rhys flopped down on the sand next to Toby. "Time flies, huh? It's way past lunchtime. No wonder I'm starving."

Toby was lying flat on his back with his eyes closed, his stomach heaving up and down. In his black, long-legged winter wetsuit, he looked pretty much like an exhausted seal.

"That was excellent." Toby spoke without opening his eyes. "I'm stoked. And that ride I got about half an hour ago – how good was that? I really nailed it. My bet's looking good – I think I might do all right in the comp. Thanks, Rhys. But I'm stuffed. Totally stuffed."

"Hey, dude, you're sounding like a surfer!" Rhys couldn't resist the tease. "Let's get some lunch – I reckon we deserve it."

"Cool. We'll wash off the boards first, then go back to the Cumberland." Toby heaved himself slowly off the sand. "Mum said she'd make some soup, and I feel like a grilled cheese sandwich, too. I'm going to grab a soak before lunch – my legs need some heat or I'll never get out there again this afternoon. I'll just get my bag."

He took a few steps, and then stopped. "Hey, seeing that we're entered in the comp, do you think they'd mind if we left our boards at the club for half an hour? Easier than hauling them over the road and back again."

"Good idea – I'll check." Rhys picked up his board. "My brother was a lifeguard here until recently. I'm sure it'll be OK. Hang on."

Rhys raced up the stone steps two at a time, with his board tucked under his arm, hoping there'd be someone in the club he might recognize. But just as he reached the door of the club, he heard Toby calling him.

"Rhys, my board bag's gone."

"No way!" Rhys ran back to the wall. He stood on the stone blocks, his feet level with Toby's head, and looked at where the bag had been. The sand was flat where it had been dragged away.

"My wax is here!" Toby held up the block of wax, which was now covered in sand. "But my board bag's gone – and my towel. I left them right here next to the wall, in line with the clock, so I'd find them easily. Do you think someone's nicked them? Who'd dare do that from right in front of the surf club?"

"I dunno." Rhys scratched his head and pushed back his hair. "But that's why I never bring anything with me – I've lost too much stuff. Don't even wear my flip-flops anymore. Let's go into the club and report it. You never know. There are lots of people around today, setting up the tents for the comp and whatever. Don't worry, Tobes – maybe someone saw who took your stuff."

Five

"So we went into the surf club." Rhys was eating lunch back at the Cumberland, and explaining to Toby's parents what had happened at the beach.

Toby hadn't said much so far, except to tell them his stuff had disappeared off the sand. But Rhys noticed Toby wasn't eating his lunch, even though they were both starving after their long session in the surf.

"And Greg – he's a lifeguard mate of my brother's – Greg said there'd been so many people putting up tents and whatever for the surfing competition that it was difficult to know who it might have been."

"Some other things have gone missing, too. Not just mine." Toby spoke quietly. "In the last few days a surfboard's been taken from the club, and a wetsuit and someone's backpack. All at different times."

No one seemed to know what to say after that. In silence, they passed around the plate of grilled ham, cheese and tomato sandwiches.

When the boys had gotten back from the beach, the Hampshires had seemed a bit shocked about Toby's stuff disappearing, but, unlike Rhys's parents if they'd been in the same situation, they'd wanted to hear the whole story, instead of going ballistic without getting all the facts.

Rhys had spent a lot of time at Toby's house over the last few months and he admired the way this family listened to each other. He lived in hope that his place would be like that once his mum was completely well. Things were heading in that direction. At least now they all sat down and had dinner together most nights – a lot of the time his mum even cooked. That was huge – much better than when Rhys had to do it on his own with no one there to eat it, except him.

"Greg reckons it's not a local." Rhys swallowed a mouthful of soup as he spoke. "It only just started happening. He said that the same thing happened in the summer. Weird, huh? It might just be coincidence, but if it was a local, it'd happen all year, wouldn't it?"

"Perhaps it *is* an out-of-towner then. Well, that narrows it down to about three or four thousand people!" Mr. Hampshire's joke broke the tension. Toby visibly relaxed and Rhys was now confident that the Hampshires would be reasonable about the whole thing. It wasn't like it was Toby's fault that his stuff had been taken.

"Do they have any leads?" Mrs. Hampshire frowned. "Surely somebody saw something."

"This is where it gets interesting." Rhys

swallowed a huge bite of his sandwich. "This is delicious, thanks, Mrs. H. So is the soup." He wiped his mouth with the back of his hand. "Anyway, apparently there was this kid on a skateboard hanging around for some of the time we were in the surf."

"That friend of yours saw him, Dad." Toby sounded a little more confident as he took up the story. "You know, the old guy who owns the surf shop? What's his name? Octopus? No, *Jellyfish*, that's it."

"*Old* guy?" Mr. Hampshire placed his hand on his chest in mock horror. "*Old* guy? You watch it, kid! Jellyfish O'Donnell is just one year older than your extremely young father! Must be all the sun and surf that's done his face in! Old guy, my hat!"

"Yeah, right." Toby grinned. "Anyway, Dad, Jellyfish said he noticed this kid near the surf club today. And yesterday there was a kid who looked the same hanging around in his shop 'acting suspiciously' – that's what he called it, didn't he, Rhys? He thinks it might be the same one who took my stuff."

Toby had some soup and a bite of sandwich, both of which he'd ignored until now. Rhys realized it was best to let Toby tell his parents the little bit they had learned from Jellyfish.

"Yesterday this kid was picking things up, walking around the shop with them and then putting them down somewhere different. Weird. There was an expensive wallet missing at the end of the day, but Jellyfish can't be sure it's the same kid – or even if he was the one who took the wallet. Could have been anyone, really – it was chaos because of the rain."

"Did Mr. O'Donnell say what the boy at the surf club looked like?" Mrs. Hampshire served both boys some more soup.

"Pretty much." Toby obviously wanted to tell his parents what he knew, so, although Rhys remembered the description exactly, he let Toby fill in the details. "He had on a black beanie, but Jellyfish said he had long blond hair. And he was wearing jeans. With a black hoodie. That's right, isn't it, Rhys?" With his mouth full of lunch, Rhys just nodded.

"Sounds like half the kids in Lorne." Mr. Hampshire sighed, and then he moved his eyes slowly from Toby to Rhys and back again, obviously searching for a solution. "What about the skateboard? There must be something that will help identify this boy."

"Yes, there is, and Jellyfish sells skateboards, so that's our best lead so far." Rhys felt he could take over here because he knew most of the stock in the surf shop so well – he spent a lot of each vacation there, checking out the surfboards and the skateboards. "He's sure it's a Speedstick. They're very expensive – and pretty rare. So the police reckon it should be quite easy to track down the skater. They've asked us to keep an eye out for it."

"But we have to phone them if we do see it." Toby had jumped in, obviously wanting to reassure his parents. "And we're only to 'follow at a distance' – that's what they said. We're not to confront the kid or anything, just watch him until they get there. The station's up the street behind the resort, so they won't have far to come."

Mrs. Hampshire frowned at her husband.

"And that's exactly what you'll do." Mr. Hampshire sounded concerned. "It's not worth getting hurt over a stolen board bag."

"We'll just get another one from Mr. O'Donnell's shop." Mrs. Hampshire smiled calmly. "And another towel. Don't take any silly risks, either of you. OK?"

Rhys looked at Toby, and Toby looked at his parents. Rhys knew that, if they did see this kid on his Speedstick, he for one would find it very hard not to confront him and demand he give back Toby's stuff. But he also knew that would be stupid. This kid might be really aggressive, maybe even dangerous, if they cornered him.

"Sure." Toby sounded totally relaxed now. "We'll be sensible, won't we, Rhys?"

"Absolutely." Rhys wouldn't do anything stupid – he was more streetwise than Toby and would make sure neither of them did anything they'd both regret. "Don't worry about us, Mrs. H. If we do see this dude, we'll call the police on my mobile and let them handle it. Mine seems to have better coverage than Toby's – his doesn't always have a signal. Anyway, we'll phone the cops. Promise. And when I promise something, that's what happens, isn't it, Toby?"

"Maybe." Toby laughed, obviously thinking about the stupid bet Rhys had made with him.

Rhys was beginning to wish he hadn't made that bet at all because Toby was getting better and better with each wave.

"Not long now till I find out, I reckon." Toby pushed Rhys in the shoulder, and a huge smile lit up his face.

This was one promise Rhys knew Toby was relying on Rhys to deliver. Rhys would die if Toby did come first or second in the Novices because then Rhys would have to do the stupid dare. What had he been thinking? Problem was he'd been desperate to be here, and coming with the Hampshires had been his only hope.

"Oh, Dad, Jellyfish said to tell you he's just as good on a board as he ever was – and that he's looking forward to the rematch." Toby grinned. "He reckons it's going to be worth waiting all these years to wipe the smile off your face once and for all. That's what he said, wasn't it, Rhys? You'd better beat him, Dad! Family pride and all that!"

"You can do it." Rhys mimicked the character in the old Adam Sandler movie they'd watched last week, but he was totally confident that Toby's dad would win the Veterans section because, from what Jellyfish had said, Mr. Hampshire had been one gnarly surfer. Rhys couldn't wait to see him compete.

Six

After lunch the two boys decided to head down to the shops and get an ice cream. That's as much as Toby had told his parents, anyway.

"You cool if we don't surf this afternoon?" Toby asked Rhys, as they went through the resort gate and down the steps to the shopping plaza. "I'm a bit sore from this morning – and losing my stuff was a real bummer."

But to Rhys it looked as though Toby had something else on his mind other than surfing – or ice cream. He had a quietly determined look on his face which Rhys had only seen a couple of times before – here in Lorne last vacation when Toby took over and organized the ambulance after the accident; and then on stage last month when Toby took the State Tap Dancing Championship for the third year in a row. Yes, he could be single-minded when something really mattered.

"Yeah, no worries – I'm good. We can hit the surf first thing tomorrow." Rhys knew he was right about Toby having an ulterior motive as they passed one ice cream shop and then another. "But where are we going?" Rhys had his own ideas about what they should do this afternoon, but it wasn't his call.

"I figured we'd go to the new skate park – check it out." Toby sounded so casual that no one else would have picked up on what he really had in mind. "You're into skating, aren't you?"

"Yeah, absolutely. I read almost as many

skateboard magazines as surfing ones – you know that. And DVDs – the footage on the new *Girl* DVD is really excellent."

"What? Not that many girls skate, do they?" Toby looked surprised.

"*Girl* is the brand name. But, yes, they do. There are even some professional female skaters. I'd really like to try it while we're here. Wish I had a board."

They crossed the road and walked along in silence until they came to the skate park. No need to talk about what they were really doing here. They sat down on a bench next to the bowl and for the next few minutes they watched the kids with boards who were skating in various parts of the park – some could hardly stand on their boards, while others seemed really talented.

Rhys ignored the younger kids and concentrated on a group of four or five older guys who were excellent skaters. Every now and then one of them pulled off something really cool and the others tapped the noses of their boards on the bowl to applaud their friend's skill. They made skating look easy.

"Toby, did you see that?" gasped Rhys. "That's way smooth. That guy just went from a 5-0 grind to a tailslide and reverted out. That's awesome. Wish I could do that."

"Yeah, and that guy on top of the ramp – what's he doing?" Toby's mouth stayed wide open.

"That's called a backside disaster." Rhys had seen skaters do it on DVD. "But he did it so smoothly! See, he rolled up to the ramp, did a backside ollie and slapped the middle of his board on the coping – then he rocked the back wheels in over the coping and rolled away." Rhys sat back and grinned. "It was so quick, wasn't it? I've seen pros do it on DVD – they'll use the wall of an empty pool or something more difficult than a ramp. But that was so cool. These skaters are great. I wonder if they're locals or not? They're so good!"

After that, Rhys didn't feel like talking. He just sat in silence and watched the awesome display of skateboarding.

"Whoa, look out, little dude," Toby yelled a few

minutes later. "Hey, Rhys, that was close! Did you see that little guy drop into the bowl? He almost got cleaned up by the older guys."

"Those little kids should look before they drop in." Rhys shook his head. "The older skaters need eyes in the back of their heads. Skating is dangerous enough without having to worry about colliding with someone who isn't paying attention. I reckon those kids would learn heaps by sitting next to the bowl like us and just watching. I know I am, but I wish I had a board."

For the next half hour, Rhys tried to forget all about the real reason he and Toby had come to the skate park, as he sat in awe and watched some of the best skaters he had ever seen.

"Sweet, man! You got heaps more air that time!" shouted an older skater, as he took a drink from his water bottle.

"Yeah. Thanks, dude." His friend nodded. "It felt good."

From where he was sitting, Rhys couldn't help but overhear the skaters' conversation as they walked away from the bowl.

"That line you took was sweet," said one, "but my kickflip to fakie is still sketchy. You go again – my legs are getting tired. That was an awesome session – it was worth the long drive. Thanks for organizing it. We'll do it again soon, huh?"

Then one of their mates did a huge boneless out of the coping and Rhys was seriously hooked. "That was gnarly." He found it impossible not to gush. "Toby, somehow I've got to get my hands on a skateboard. Maybe Jellyfish has a used one at the shop that I could borrow – maybe your dad could ask him. It's *so* like surfing – without the waves! Now that Mum's getting better, I could skate when I'm back home in the city, instead of being totally frustrated because I can't get to the surf. I *so* want to skate."

He leaned back against the seat and formulated a plan. "Maybe I could persuade my brother to help me build a mini-ramp in our backyard – he's pretty handy with that sort of stuff. Cool idea, huh? I reckon my dad would help, too. He likes building things. And you could use it, too."

"Definitely sounds like a plan." There was a note of hesitation in Toby's voice. "But somehow we need to get skateboards first! No good having a ramp if we don't have boards."

"Hey!" Rhys suddenly felt really excited. "Guess what the prize is for the Junior Surf champ? It's a gift certificate for the surf shop – I could get a skateboard. Cool. I'd totally forgotten. Even more reason to win!"

Several more minutes passed with Rhys entranced by the skaters and oblivious to whatever else was going on around him. He was floating in skateboard heaven.

"Rhys, isn't that Braddon Lynch over there?" Toby startled Rhys out of his gnarly daydream.

"Braddon? On a skateboard? You're kidding, right?" But Rhys could see that it was definitely Braddon, and he was unfortunately heading in their direction, although Rhys was confident that the loser hadn't seen them – yet!

"Toby, don't look at him and he might not see

us." Rhys slunk down into the seat and pulled his hood over his head and face. He hoped to slip under the radar – kind of like when he was little and he used to hide from his big brother by putting his hands over his eyes. It didn't work then – and it didn't work now!

"Too late – he's coming over." Toby laughed, turning his back to Braddon and winking at Rhys. "Not our day, as Dad would say! But, hey – maybe you can borrow his skateboard. That'd be a plus." Toby screwed up his face at Rhys, before he put on a fake smile and turned around towards Braddon Lynch.

"Yeah, as if he'd share with me." Rhys remembered the previous night when Braddon had seemed like such a loser. "I didn't get one chip last night at dinner. Not one – and neither did you, dude."

But then Rhys knew immediately that he'd been too harsh and he felt guilty for talking like that. OK, so he didn't want to get involved with Braddon Lynch, but he wondered if Braddon was a loner because his mother *did* have a problem? Maybe he couldn't cope with stuff at home – Rhys knew what that was like.

"Not long now," Toby whispered. "Ten, nine, eight ..."

While Toby kept counting down, Rhys desperately searched for a positive in what could be an awkward situation. He figured that skateboarding might give him and Braddon a connection that they hadn't had last night. Stranger things had happened – like Toby becoming his friend, against all the odds. Maybe Rhys should start again and get to know Braddon, before he leapt to any more conclusions. And, hey, if Braddon would lend them his skateboard while they were getting to know each other, then that'd be good, too, wouldn't it?

Seven

"Hey, Braddon." Rhys decided to forget about last night. "You didn't tell us you're a skater."

"How could I?" snapped Braddon. "My father thinks only ferals and street kids skate. That's why we were late for dinner last night. He went off – delivered another one of his stupid lectures. It's pathetic. He thinks surfing is more acceptable than skating."

Rhys was stunned by this outburst and had no idea what to say, so he was relieved when Braddon continued talking. "He's gone back to the city for work – that's the only reason I'm out here with my board. I hid it in my bag to get it down to Lorne. He'd go crazy if he found out I hadn't gotten rid of it. It's so lame. You'd think I was doing drugs or something, the way he carries on. I don't want to surf, I want to skate … And my friends call me *Brad*." The bitter tone of his voice was disturbing.

Last night Braddon hadn't talked to them at all, but just now he'd hardly taken a breath as he spat out his impassioned monologue like a seasoned politician. Away from his parents, he was a totally different person.

"Right." Rhys hesitated a second as he struggled to process what he'd just heard. "Yeah. *Brad*. Sounds good."

Mr. Lynch had seemed so nice compared to his wife. Rhys was shocked that he'd been right that Brad had tough stuff in his life – but he was way off the mark as to why. And Rhys felt guilty –

he'd made up his mind about Brad without getting to know him first. He should have known better – much better. Good one, Rhys.

"That really sucks." Rhys meant it. "Sorry, dude. We had no idea."

Toby seemed equally stunned, but instead of helping Rhys sort it out, Toby just walked away without saying anything and sat down on a nearby wall, ignoring Rhys and Brad as he watched the skaters on the vert ramp. He obviously had other things on his mind.

Wondering how he could make things up to Brad, Rhys thought he might as well just go for it. "Listen, I've never spent much time on a skateboard. Could you give me a lesson? Teach me some stuff? I kind of know the basics – and I've been watching these older dudes for a while, so I've got some idea."

"Really? You want *me* to teach *you*?" Brad seemed genuinely pleased, as he nervously pushed back his straight blond hair and tucked it behind his ears. "Are you serious? I mean I thought you were a champion surfer. Do you really want to skate?" After the initial enthusiasm he suddenly seemed wary, like he thought Rhys was setting him up.

"Yeah, I'm serious. And I'm not a surfing champion – yet! That's in a couple of days!" Rhys laughed, trying to sound totally relaxed because for two major reasons he desperately wanted Brad to believe him.

First, he felt guilty that he'd been so quick to jump to the wrong conclusion about Brad last night, and, second, because he wanted to ride a skateboard, right now, this minute – and Brad had one.

"Watching these guys, I reckon skating kind of crosses over with surfing." Rhys was trying not to sound too anxious. "Mind if I take a turn?"

Brad looked at him and shrugged. "Sure. Why not? Let's see what you can do." Brad grinned as he slammed his foot onto the board so that it jumped into his hand. He passed it to Rhys. "If you do OK, we'll go over to a fun box. You're a surfer – I reckon you could handle that. Let's see your stuff."

Brad showed Rhys a few moves and Rhys

practiced up and down the path with a fair amount of success. This was great. He could do it – in fact, it was easy.

Then, as Brad began to explain some of the more difficult skateboarding techniques to Rhys, Toby suddenly seemed to become interested, too and pushed his way in between them. For some weird reason Toby looked a bit aggressive.

"What's the problem, Tobes?" Rhys wondered if Toby was angry that Rhys and Brad were getting along so well. Surely not. They were best friends, but they both had other friends, too.

"Hey, Brad." Toby totally ignored Rhys's question. "That skateboard of yours. It looks really different from all the other boards around here – pretty flash. What brand is it?"

"It's a Speedstick." Brad proudly blurted out the answer, seeming oblivious to the sinister connotations. He smiled as he flipped his skateboard over and showed it off. "How cool is it? I bought it on the Internet when they were released in the States. I've only seen one other since. They're just hitting the shops in the city here now, but I've had mine for a couple of months. Yeah, definitely the best board I've ever used. It cost me a fortune – but it's worth it."

Rhys felt his lungs tighten, as though someone had just put a belt around his chest and pulled it hard. Trying not to look obvious, he checked out what Brad was wearing – a dark long-sleeved T-shirt and jeans. He didn't have a black hoodie with him, or a beanie, but maybe he'd taken them off or something. And his hair matched the description, too.

Great – what were they supposed to do now? Call the cops? Mr. Hampshire would be really impressed if they accused his boss's son of theft without any proof. That wouldn't be a smart move. They needed some actual evidence first. And somehow Rhys had to talk to Toby about it, without Brad realizing that they were on to him – *if* he were the thief, which, for some reason, Rhys doubted. He couldn't explain it – it was just a gut feeling.

"You coming or what?" asked Brad. He gently

pushed his board back and forth with one foot, and nodded in the direction of the fun box. Then, ignoring Toby, he pushed off and rolled away from Rhys. He really knew how to control that board.

"Yeah. Yeah, I'm coming." Rhys stumbled over the words, but hoped he'd sounded normal. He was really confused. Then he lowered his voice and spoke conspiratorially to Toby who, having made the discovery, was standing stunned.

"We need to go along with this for a while." Rhys was trying to make sense of the situation. "Find out a bit more first. I just can't see Brad being the thief - it doesn't make sense. Maybe he'll take me back to his place later and I can snoop around or something. I've got a feeling it's not him. Innocent until proven guilty, right?"

And then Rhys's mobile rang, so he raised his hand in Brad's direction, holding up his phone for a moment, before he answered it. "Hey, Mr. H. Really? You're kidding. In a boat shed? OK, cool. I'll let Toby know - he's right here. Yep. See you then. Bye." And he slipped his mobile back into the pocket on the leg of his jeans. "Your dad said he tried your phone and it didn't work. Anyway, the police have found a stack of stolen stuff in a boat shed below one of those houses along the ridge walk. And we have to meet your parents at the police station at four, so you can see if your bag and towel are there. Cool, yeah?"

"Yeah, but, hey, didn't Mrs. Lynch say that's where their house is? Yes! Braddon's house is up there on the ridge walk!" Toby's eyes seemed to widen with the anticipation of a major bust. "Sounds like it's a sure thing. He doesn't know the police have found the stolen goods, so he might go up there when you've finished your session. Who knows? Stick with him, Rhys. He doesn't seem dangerous. I'll hang out here and see what happens."

Unconvinced, Rhys just nodded and ran over to Brad who was sitting on a bench, his feet on his board, impatiently rolling it back and forth.

"Sorry!" Rhys patted the mobile in his pocket, as though this would be enough explanation. "The parents!" No need to mention whose parents, or why they were phoning.

"OK, let's do this." Brad seemed pleased that Rhys was keen to skate, and obviously wasn't worried about the phone call, which had to be a good thing, didn't it?

And so Rhys had his first skateboarding lesson on a Speedstick which, if Toby were right, could be owned by a blatant thief – a rich kid, who could easily afford to buy all the stuff that had been stolen. See, it didn't make any sense. Why would Brad be the thief?

Brad wouldn't steal surfing stuff anyway – he didn't want to surf. He'd made that very obvious – so why would he steal a surfboard? This was whacked. Something wasn't right – the pieces didn't fit. There had to be another solution. But what?

Eight

"Hey, Brad, show me that again, will you?" Rhys had mastered some of the moves on Brad's skateboard during the last hour, but he was keen to learn as much as he could now, just in case the lesson came to an abrupt halt. "I don't get that kick bit. Can you do it again? Which is the front – and which is the back? It's not like my surfboard where the back's the end with the fin!"

"Have you seen those surfboards that are kind of like skateboards?" Brad was smiling as though they were friends sharing an ordinary afternoon's skating session. "You're awesome for a beginner – guess that's because you're a surfer. I reckon you need some of the same skills for skating as you do for surfing. And those new boards kind of put the two together."

Rhys was amazed that Brad was so chatty and seemed pretty normal. And he was fun to hang out with. If he *were* the surf club thief, he'd be nervous about being found out, wouldn't he? Now that he'd spent some time with Brad, Rhys was sure he wasn't the person that Rhys and Toby had first thought. But the Speedstick pointed to guilt. Maybe Jellyfish had been wrong about the board.

"Anyway," Brad continued animatedly, "they're called something else – not just surfboards – but I can't remember what, and they're different from normal boards because both ends are the same shape. And they've got three fins at each end; there's no definite back or front, so you can surf in either direction. It's manic – like extreme surfing. They do aerial and skateboard-type tricks in the surf: 360s, ollies and kickflips! Now that's the sort of surfing I'd like to watch. Do you know what I'm talking about?"

"Yeah, they're awesome." Rhys knew exactly what they were – he'd read about them in a magazine recently. "They're called *twin-tails* – reversible surfboards. I saw a couple of guys using them here last vacation. In fact, that's one of the prizes for the senior section in the Easter Surf comp. Pretty cool, huh? Mr. Hampshire might win it!"

They skated together for another fifteen minutes or so, until Rhys noticed Toby frantically waving him over.

"Hang on, Brad – looks like Toby wants something. You have your turn. I'll take a break and see what's going down with Toby. Thanks, dude, that was excellent. Wait for me, OK?"

As he pushed the board gently towards Brad with his right foot, Rhys hoped he'd sounded normal. This was so confusing. Being nice to Brad was easy. He was an excellent skater and fun to hang out with – and of course, using Brad's special-edition skateboard was awesome.

"What's up, Tobes?" Rhys was hoping this wouldn't take long – he wanted to get back to skating.

Whatever it was, Toby was acting strangely. He was looking at Brad, but then turning around to look at a skater on the vert ramp, and then looking back at Brad again. Back and forth, back and forth. Rhys was surprised his head didn't just topple off and plonk onto the pavement. What on earth was he doing?

"So, what have you found out? Is it Brad, or what?" Rhys was really enjoying his session with Brad, and the more time he spent with him, the more convinced he was that Brad's only crime was riding a skateboard without his father's permission.

"You need to see this!" And then, without waiting for Rhys, Toby strode off towards the ramp where a skater about their age was enjoying a session on his own. The older guys had left and some younger kids were standing around watching the awesome display. "He's a brilliant skater, but here's the thing – remember Brad said he'd only seen one other Speedstick? Well, check out this guy's board!" Toby pointed with his eyes, rather than making an obvious hand movement. "Well?"

"It's definitely a Speedstick!" Rhys was amazed. The underside of the board was a dead giveaway. "I thought they were rare – and there's two in this one skate park, right this minute! How's that possible?"

"Beats me." Toby shrugged and leaned back against a wall. "This gets weirder and weirder. Now we have two suspects – both with Speedsticks, and both with dark clothes and blond hair. So, here's the thing – we need to sort this. You stick with Brad. And I'll stay with this dude. We'll just kind of keep an eye on them and see what happens. OK? If one of them is the thief, they might just give themselves away somehow. You cool with that?"

"Yeah, but I don't think it's Brad. He's got no reason to steal – and he's really fun when you get to know him. And an awesome skater. But, hey, what if one or both of them leave the park? What should we do then?" Rhys was worried because of the promise they'd made to Toby's parents. "Should we follow them? And call the police? Or what? If your guy's the one, he might be dangerous."

"I'm not stupid. I'm just going to follow him, that's all. We can text each other if things get tricky. OK?" Toby seemed totally focused on solving this. "My phone's got a signal. My sister just sent me a text. She's coming down after all – day after tomorrow – and bringing another girl, a friend from school. Boring! They'll take over the place – that's what girls do." Rhys noticed him glance up from his mobile, obviously keeping an eye on his suspect. "Um, Rhys, talking of girls – check out the skater!"

"What the …" Rhys couldn't believe his eyes. The black beanie had gone and long blond hair tumbled down the back of the dark T-shirt. "Seems we got that wrong, too. That skater is a chick!"

Toby frowned at Rhys. "This is whacked. What's going to happen next? Anyway, you stick with Brad and I'll follow this chick – don't think I'll be in any danger." He laughed awkwardly and then looked serious again. "OK, take it easy and text me if there's anything going down. If Jellyfish is right, one of these two has to be the thief."

"You're really into this, aren't you?" Rhys was amazed how seriously Toby was taking the whole thing. "You've been watching too many cop shows on TV! And don't worry about me; Brad won't be a problem – trust me. Whatever happens, I'll meet you at the police station at four. Stay cool." And, wondering how this would all turn out, he jogged towards the fun box, ready to continue his lesson.

But, by the time Rhys got there, Brad had disappeared. No way! He had to be here somewhere. Rhys quickly scanned the entire skate park. No Brad. Rhys checked his options and on a hunch took off towards Mountjoy Parade. Where would Brad go? Home? OK, if he were heading towards the ridge walk, he'd go past the Beachside Cinema, right?

And that's exactly where Rhys spotted him. Brad had stopped outside the old-fashioned movie theater and was picking up a copy of the same sheet

Rhys had gotten that morning. It listed the movie titles and times of screenings. That seemed pretty innocent. It wasn't like he was running away – but why had he left so abruptly? Weirder and weirder. Nothing here made any sense at all – and they were no closer to finding their thief. Or were they?

Nine

Rhys had to make sure he kept completely out of sight as he followed Brad along the ridge walk path above the beach. He hadn't thought about it too much, but he was a little apprehensive about the discoveries he might make by following Brad. Was he really the thief – or was it that girl from the skate park? Rhys was hoping it wasn't Brad.

At the start of the ridge walk, there was a picket gate, which Rhys had never seen closed – it just hung on its hinges, creaking in the breeze. Here the path was cleared and straight – it would be difficult not to be seen if Brad turned around, so he hung back behind the gate until Brad disappeared from view.

The first few properties were separated from the path by tea tree fencing – thin sticks in tall bundles, bound together with wire. The fences here were so high that Rhys couldn't see over the top of them, although over the years he'd checked out lots of those backyards with his brother, when they'd been looking for things to do during vacations. Nothing quite like a good dare, although he'd prefer to forget about dares for the moment!

As Brad walked around a corner some way along the track, Rhys hurried to catch up. From there the path began to wind around the hill and it was quite overgrown with tall bendy trees, as well as a variety of short, thick bushes – probably the only things that would survive so close to the ocean.

Now that he was able to follow Brad more

closely without the fear of being seen, Rhys's heart rate settled down, although he was still a bit apprehensive. He couldn't help it – he liked Brad now that he'd spent a bit of time with him. But you could never be sure what someone was really like – you kind of had to trust that they were who they said they were, didn't you?

It seemed strange to Rhys that he and Brad had been getting along so well at the skate park – and then Brad had left without saying goodbye. Maybe he'd decided that he didn't want to share his brilliant board with Rhys after all – or maybe, when he thought about it, Brad had suspected that Rhys and Toby might tell his parents about him still having his Speedstick. There was no way either of them would rat on him – but he didn't know that, did he? Or maybe he *was* the thief after all. No, that didn't seem possible.

The path here was dappled with sunlight. Dark shadows thrown by the taller trees made it quite difficult to see up ahead. There were branches reaching awkwardly across the path and some of them hung down low, making it a bit of an obstacle course. Even so, Rhys had no trouble keeping up with Brad, who suddenly took a sharp left off the track and headed away from the houses down towards the ocean. Was he going to a boat shed – *the* boat shed?

Rhys took a deep breath. Don't be stupid, Brad's not the thief – he's probably just … just what? Rhys couldn't think what Brad might be doing. If this were his family's property, shouldn't he be heading up the hill towards the house? OK, calmness. Just follow him and you'll find out what he's doing. There'll be a simple answer, you know that. Friendship starts with trust – so where's the trust, Rhys?

But then, before he could get his hands out in front to stop himself, Rhys had fallen heavily and his head hit the ground with a sickening thud.

"Arrgghhh! Help me!" Rhys wasn't sure if the words actually came out of his mouth or if he'd just thought them. He was totally disoriented, so he lay still, wondering what on earth had just happened. His head was thumping so badly, it felt like he'd been whacked with something.

Whoa, that hurt. He tried to get up, but quickly decided against it. The ground was spinning and he felt a bit nauseous. He touched his head where it hurt most, but there didn't seem to be any blood, although he was sure it must have a huge dent in it.

Then he could hear a sort of drumming noise. Was that the thumping in his head? No – someone was running along the path towards him. He hoped they could help him.

"Hey, you OK?" The voice sounded familiar. It took a bit of focusing, but then he knew – it was Toby. "What happened?" Toby helped Rhys to sit up against a tree. At least the path wasn't revolving the way it had been at first.

"I'm not sure." Rhys knew his voice sounded strange, but he couldn't help that. "I was following Brad – and then I fell. I think – I don't know really. What are you doing here?"

"I followed that skater chick up the hill, but she disappeared while I was hiding near that gate at the start of the path." Toby looked concerned. "Are you sure you're OK? The hospital's just down the hill – I passed it on my way here."

"No, I'm fine. A bit dizzy, that's all." Rhys put his hand to his head. "I just need to sit here for a couple of minutes. So where did she go – the skater chick?"

"I'm not sure." Toby was obviously puzzled. "How could she have vanished off the path like that? I wasn't that far behind her."

"Those brush fences – some of them have gates." Rhys was finding it hard to think clearly, but he knew the area well. He'd hung out here with his brother since he was little. "You'd never notice them – got to know what to look for. Maybe she opened one – went inside. Maybe she lives there." He felt his brain gradually freeing itself from the fog.

"Sounds possible." Toby still looked worried. "Forget about her for now – we can check her out later. She'll go back to the skate park sometime. No rush. You sure you're OK?"

"Yeah, I'm fine – just a bit dizzy, that's all. And my head thumps." He felt for the lump he was sure had to be there, but it all seemed OK. "Boy, that hurt."

"What actually happened? Can you remember?"

"Well, I was following Brad – and he went down the hill just here, I think." Rhys struggled to get it right. "It feels like someone hit me with something, but that doesn't seem likely. I must have tripped over a rock. Can you see anything?"

Toby scanned the area close to where Rhys was sitting.

"Here's your attacker!" Toby laughed as he kicked his foot against something. "There's a tree root sticking up out of the path like a loop – you must have caught your foot and hit your head on the ground. Is your foot OK? You've got the comp the day after tomorrow. Try and stand up – put some weight on it."

"It's a bit sore!" Rhys winced as he put his foot on the ground, but the pain wasn't too bad. "It's not broken or anything – I can walk on it. See?" And he hobbled over to look at his woody assailant. "Didn't see that one coming, did I? Anyway, I'll be fine. We can ice it later. But we're here now, so let's check out the boat shed and see what Brad's up to. You game?"

"You kidding?" Toby smiled at Rhys. "Of course I'm game. This is one mystery I'd really like to solve. Why would he go to the boat shed, unless he's up to something? Look, there's a dirt track down the hill. Let's take a look."

But as the boat shed came into view, Rhys could hear voices.

"Quick – in here!" He pulled Toby into a thick clump of bushes, which covered them completely.

The boat shed door was wide open – and there were three shadows inside.

Ten

"So what are you doing here?" It was Brad's voice – Rhys was sure of that. "This isn't your place – you shouldn't be here."

The reply was so muffled that Rhys couldn't hear the answer.

"Leave my brother alone." It was a girl's voice and she sounded almost hysterical. "Come on, Jason – we're out of here. All the stuff's gone anyway –

there's no point staying. Come on!"

And then the skater chick pulled what Rhys assumed was her brother by the arm out of the boat shed and into full view.

"It's her," whispered Toby. "And check out her brother – black beanie, blond hair, jeans, black hoodie – and that's the Speedstick under his arm. She must have borrowed it! We've got him!"

"But whose place is this?" Rhys wondered out loud. "And why is Brad here?"

"Only one way to find out." And with that Toby stood up and walked boldly towards the boat shed.

"Wait up – we're supposed to ..." But Rhys had to hobble after him so that Toby didn't do this alone. When he saw the surprised look on all three faces, he really wished he had a camera.

"So, Brad, you need any help?" Toby asked assertively.

"Whoa! What's going on here?" Jason, the girl's brother, looked as though he were about to make a run for it.

"Hang on a minute." Toby, although about the

same age as the other boy, was a bit taller than him, so he was able to grab his arm, push it up behind his back and hold him firmly.

"OK, Brad, let's start with you." Rhys wanted confirmation that Brad wasn't the thief. "You left the skate park pretty suddenly. Why are you here?"

"Sorry I skipped off like that, Rhys." Brad looked upset. "Mum phoned and told me to meet her at a cafe in town. She couldn't see me with the board, so I raced back here to hide it. This is Shiloh's place. After what Mum said last night about no one staying here while she's away, I figured this would be the safest place to leave my board; my parents wouldn't bother to check the shed – no reason to – so they wouldn't find it." He looked really confused. "But when I got here, the shed was unlocked and *he* was already inside." Brad pointed at Jason. "And then *she* arrived a few minutes later. What do you reckon they're doing here? They're trespassing, I know that much."

"So are you, ferret head." Jason struggled in a futile attempt to get away from Toby. "This isn't your place either." Toby increased the pressure on Jason's arm so that he stopped moving and didn't bother saying anything else.

"My parents are keeping an eye on it for the owner while she's away – not that it's any of *your* business." Brad was sounding more in control now that he had backup. "So, what *are* you doing here?"

"None of your beeswax, ferret head." Jason wasn't going anywhere while Toby had hold of him, but he obviously wasn't going to cooperate either.

"I can answer that." Rhys smiled confidently at Toby and then at Brad. "But first we need to make a phone call." He felt for his mobile – but his pocket was empty. "No! I took it out when I was at the skate park – remember, Brad? You warned me about phones getting damaged if you fall on them – and I forgot to pick it up. I left it on the ground near the fun box. It'll be long gone by now."

And then a mobile began to ring.

"That's my ring tone." Rhys was stunned as "Wipeout" resonated from where the skater chick was standing. "*You've* got my phone!"

"Yeah, she's always nicking stuff." Jason eye-balled his sister. Perhaps he was trying to switch the attention from himself and implicate her for the other thefts, too. "Like that wallet you got for Dad. No way you paid for that. Go on, Stacey, admit it – you nicked that phone, didn't ya?"

Without needing to hear her reply, Rhys snatched his phone out of Stacey's hand and answered it.

"Hello. Yes. Mr. H? Is it that late? We got held up. Sorry, Mr. H, I was just about to call. Could you tell them we're at Shiloh's boat shed? Yes, that's the one – just off the ridge walk path. Yes, Toby's here, but he's a bit busy. No, his phone didn't ring, which was lucky – I'll explain later. OK? Yes, thanks, Mr. H. See you."

"It's four fifteen." Rhys knew Toby would understand without his giving away what he'd just organized with Mr. Hampshire. Toby's parents had kept the appointment at the police station and were wondering why the two boys were so late. Just as well Stacey had stolen his mobile. Funny how things worked out sometimes!

"Excellent!" Toby tightened his grip on Jason.

"So, Jason, you haven't told us why you're here." Rhys kept smiling at Brad and Toby, hoping that he sounded much calmer than he actually felt. "We'd all like to hear your story, wouldn't we, guys?"

It would probably take ten minutes for the adults to get there, although of course Brad had no idea what was going on, or that the police were on their way. Hopefully Toby could hold Jason till then.

"What were you doing in Shiloh's boat shed?" Brad demanded.

"Some feral's stolen my stuff." Jason put on a good performance, obviously hoping that Toby would let him go once he'd explained the situation. "I had my surfboard here and some other stuff. The comp's the day after tomorrow – and now someone's nicked it. And a backpack full of expensive wax and things."

"It's not *his* surfboard." Stacey blurted out her accusation, while Jason tried unsuccessfully to get

Toby to release him.

"Shut up, Stace – don't say nothing." Jason looked really angry as he wrestled with Toby.

"He stole it from the surf club." It seemed nothing was going to stop Stacey, now that Jason had accused her of stealing. "He wanted to go in the Easter Surf and he didn't have a board, 'cause the stupid jerk sold his board *and mine*, didn't he? *And* both our skateboards – to buy the Speedstick. I told him he couldn't. I'm his twin sister, but he still wouldn't listen to me, would he? Oh no. What's the good of one board for the two of us – and no surfboards? It sucks. There's nothing else to do in this town."

Rhys and Toby exchanged a knowing glance, although Brad, who had no idea what she was talking about, now looked even more confused than he had before.

"Did he now?" boomed a deep voice, coming up behind them. "That's very interesting, young lady. We'd like you and your brother to accompany us down to the police station to assist with our enquiries into a stash of stolen goods that was retrieved from this very boat shed earlier today, some of which belongs to this young man, we believe."

He stepped towards Toby and patted him on the shoulder.

"Thanks. Toby, is it? We'll take over from here. You've done a great job. Well done, son. And well done to you, too, Rhys. You'd make excellent detectives."

Toby dropped Jason's arm and stretched the fingers on the hand that had been restraining him.

"Thanks." Toby sounded relieved. "How did you get here so quickly?"

"Just lucky – we were out on patrol on this side of town," explained the policeman, "and when we took the call from the station we knew exactly where you were. Your father's coming to pick you up in a moment, Toby, so we'll see you all back at the station. Well done to the three of you, gentlemen."

And with that he and his partner took the twins up the hill to where Rhys imagined their patrol car was parked, somewhere above the ridge walk path.

"So, Brad, thanks for that – if I hadn't followed you here … well, we might never have found out who'd stolen Toby's stuff off the beach. So thanks." Rhys didn't want to go into the fact that Brad had been a sort of suspect, so he quickly moved on. "Don't think you should leave your board here though – I reckon the three of us should talk to your dad about us all wanting to skateboard."

"And maybe if that doesn't work, my dad could convince him." Toby sounded confident. "Do you want a lift back to town when Dad gets here? You don't want to be too late for your mum, do you?"

"Yeah, thanks." Brad sounded hesitant. "That'd be good – and talking to them is worth a try. I'll start with Mum. But why *did* you follow me, Rhys?"

"I, er, just wanted to thank you for the lesson." It was all Rhys could think of, but it didn't sound convincing. "No, that's not entirely true. To be honest, the police told us to look out for a kid with a Speedstick. We were sure it wasn't you. Then we saw Stacey on Jason's board, so Toby followed her because we thought she was the thief. But we were wrong about her, weren't we?"

This was one uncomfortable moment, so Rhys rushed on.

"Your Speedstick is so cool – I know now why that kid Jason was so desperate to have one – it's amazing. Thanks for letting me use yours. Hey, why don't the three of us catch that movie tonight – you know, the extreme surfing one at Beachside Cinema. I heard its got some twin-tails action. What do you reckon? Toby, you up for it?"

Brad seemed unsure, his eyes darting from Rhys to Toby and then back to Rhys again.

"Excellent." Toby sounded so normal that Rhys envied him. "We could grab some fish and chips on the way and then go see the movie. What time's it start?"

It was as though the three of them had always been friends and this was something they often did together.

"Hang on, I've got the movie page here." Brad pulled a crumpled sheet out of his pocket. "I'm dying to see it. I love watching surfing movies – just don't want to actually surf. Thought I'd be going to the movie on my own – the parentals aren't interested! Shocking, right?"

Rhys laughed with Brad, and then Toby joined in. Last night Rhys had been so certain that he and Toby would never want to hang out with Braddon Lynch – things had really changed since then.

"But now that you've convinced me how good skating is, I've got to get you surfing." Rhys took the movie page from Brad and checked the starting time. "And, Toby, we might even pick up some gnarly stuff from the film that'll help us in the comp. Bring it on."

Eleven

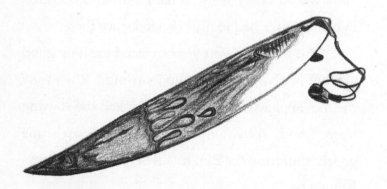

"Hey, Toby, don't you reckon it's a bit weird, the way that boat's been hanging off the point all afternoon?" Rhys and Toby had been in the surf since lunch, doing their final practice session before the comp the following day. "No one's fishing from it. Anyway, it's the wrong spot – fish don't bite there."

"Seems a bit suspect." Toby paddled his board

around and just stared at the yacht. "I've been watching it since it anchored – I wonder what they're up to … There's been no one up on deck for hours. Maybe they're drug smugglers."

Rhys thought his friend was making a joke, but, as they waited for a decent wave, Toby continued his crazy theory. "I've read about stuff like that happening off the coast." Toby frowned, obviously trying to remember something. "Customs Watch – that's what it's called. They had their van down in the parking lot last trip – remember? I read a pamphlet that said the Water Police and Customs are always on the lookout for boats that might be importing or distributing illegal drugs. They caught some guys doing that here in Lorne a few years ago – it was further around though, near the mouth of the river, I think. Yeah, they could be smugglers."

Rhys spun his board around and looked at the boat again, but there was still no sign of anyone. And now that it was getting dark it was even more odd because there was no light shining from the galley.

"Hey, maybe those people on the boat are

waiting till it's pitch black before they use that dinghy to smuggle stuff ashore." Toby was definitely getting into this. "Could be drugs – could be anything!"

"Now you're the one making assumptions and sounding paranoid." Rhys laughed as he pointed his board towards the shore and looked back over his shoulder to check out the next set. "You've definitely watched too many of those crime shows on TV! Hey, I've had enough waves for today. What about you, Tobes? Can we make this the last one?"

It was actually getting pretty dark now, so it was definitely time to get out of the water. Funny, Rhys wasn't cold, even though his hands could feel the water temperature was dropping rapidly. The sun had gone behind the hill about an hour ago.

Obviously his adrenalin had already started to pump – tomorrow he'd be competing in the Easter Surf. He had to win – he had to – he'd be the Junior Surf champion and the owner of a brand new skateboard. Yes!

"OK, you coming, dude? This one will do." Rhys started to paddle fast to catch the wave.

And together he and Toby enjoyed the last wave of the day – just the two of them, with no one else around except a couple of surfers who'd ridden the last set and were now walking slowly up the beach towards the surf club.

As he and Toby were wading through the shallows, on impulse Rhys turned around and took another look at the solitary yacht. It was quite dark now, but there was still no light onboard. That *was* weird. Then something moved on the deck.

"Hey, Tobes. Look! There's someone getting into that dinghy."

They watched as the dinghy's bowline was released from the yacht by a dark, shadowy figure. Rhys found it impossible to see properly. There could have been two or three people, but it was too dark to be certain.

"They're heading in to shore and going around the point." Toby sounded excited. "They might be going to one of the boat sheds near Brad's place. Let's phone him when we get back to the Cumberland. He might want to check it out."

"Get real!" Rhys shuddered involuntarily. "If there is something going down, Brad's better off not knowing about it. A stolen surfboard and stuff is one thing – but smuggling drugs is totally different. Like you said, that's what Customs and the Water Police are for – it's their job. Let's forget it, OK? It's probably nothing anyway."

Toby just shrugged without answering, so Rhys kept talking, letting the tension drop naturally. "These stairs are so easy on the way down – but they seem much steeper going home after a long session in the surf, don't they?" It was lame, but it was good enough to do the trick and soon Toby was whistling something unrecognizable, probably something from his tap class.

Rhys felt they'd had enough drama already this week – if someone was doing something they shouldn't, Rhys really didn't want to know. He had to concentrate on the comp – that's what he was here for, not to solve an endless number of supposed mysteries.

Rhys and Toby walked on with the thumping

of the surf behind them a constant reminder of what lay ahead of them in the morning.

"Hey, Rhys, isn't that Jason and Stacey on the other side of the road?" Toby pointed at the path that led to the ridge walk. "Where do you reckon they're going? Bit dark for a jog, isn't it?"

"Will you stop?" Rhys laughed. Toby just shrugged.

"Well, if you want my candid opinion, Detective Toby," Rhys mimicked a Sherlock Holmes voice, "then I'd say that the armfuls of something they're carrying is – no, not stolen goods as first suspected by my learned colleague, but – wait for it – yes, I'm definitely onto them now; on closer examination, that's takeout food they're smuggling up the path. Yes, it's confirmed, they're taking pizza home for dinner!"

Rhys was laughing so much that he had to juggle his surfboard and grasp it tightly to avoid dropping it. "You fool! Their house is up on the ridge walk – the policeman told us that yesterday when we got your board bag and towel back. Their dad's a fisherman and they live in a house above the co-op where he works." Toby still looked unconvinced. "You're hopeless, Tobes. Will you give it a rest? We're not the Famous Five, or the Secret Seven! For starters there's just two of us. We're surfers – and we've got to concentrate on the comp. It's tomorrow, in case you've forgotten!"

Toby started to laugh, too, as they trudged the short distance up the steep hill and into the entrance of the resort. That was the thing about Toby – he never took himself so seriously that he couldn't laugh at himself.

"Some heat will be so good!" Toby led the way to the pool area, not giving any more time to his ridiculous theories.

Rhys and Toby stood under the outside shower with their boards and washed off the salt water. Then, taking no chances, they left their boards and wetsuits where they could see them, and slipped into the soothing heat of the Jacuzzi.

"This is excellent!" Rhys leaned back against the wall. "After a session in the surf, I'm used to walking right up that steep hill to the grandparents' place and having a warm shower, if my brother hasn't used all the hot water before I get there! Staying so close to the beach, and having a Jacuzzi, is awesome."

"And Mum's making her special pasta for dinner." Toby was so relaxed now that he was in the warm water that he seemed to have forgotten all about the supposed drug smugglers. "That's what she always does the night before I dance in comps or concerts – carbs are great for energy. But you know that, right?" Rhys just nodded that he did.

"Anyway, I love Mum's spaghetti – she makes this amazing tomato sauce with meatballs and kind of flaky meat – but you know that, too. You've had it before, haven't you? So we're sure to win tomorrow!" He smiled and closed his eyes, leaning back against the hot water jets.

"Do you reckon Brad will come to the comp?" Rhys asked his question before he slipped under the steaming water for a second, coming up to comment. "He really enjoyed the movie last night – and he seemed pretty keen about watching us, didn't he?"

"Yeah, I reckon he'll be there." Toby frowned. "He's pretty cool once you get to know him, isn't he? I'll give him a call after dinner and see if he wants to meet us at the surf club before our first round."

"Cool." Rhys thought about it. "You know, I reckon that the three of us are getting along pretty well now. Who knows? We might even hang out together once we're back in the city." He frowned and then remembered what he'd been talking about. "Anyway, tomorrow! If Brad gets there a bit earlier we could warm up on his skateboard. That board of his is awesome, and after that session this morning, I'm really getting the hang of it. Yeah, he's cool – we should ask him over tomorrow night to celebrate our victories!"

Rhys moved around so that the warm jets of water could bubble into his tired legs. He closed his eyes for a while until he remembered something he'd totally forgotten until now. "Hey, Tobes, Dad gave me some money to take everyone to dinner one night." He smiled, recalling his dad's unexpected offer. For once his dad had been interested in his surfing and he'd been keen to know all about the competition. His parents had even thought about coming down to watch him, but his mum still wasn't really well enough to do that – maybe next year.

"We could all go to the Seaside Palace, if you want. The food's even better when you eat it there." Rhys had happy memories of eating at the local Chinese restaurant on the last day of every vacation, until a few years ago when his mum had gotten so sick that it just wasn't possible anymore.

"Let's focus on the comp first, huh?" Toby splashed Rhys with a handful of froth, sank into the bubbles and then resurfaced. "Before we go crazy organizing a victory dinner, we have to win! Or had you forgotten that?"

Twelve

"Hey, Brad! Yeah, we were going to call you." Rhys nodded at Toby and pointed at his mobile. "Yeah, we've just finished dinner. Mrs. H made the best pasta ever! So, what's up? You coming down to the surf club in the morning? What time can you meet us ... What? When? You're joking! What did you see ... Not much in the dark, huh? Really? Hang on,

Toby wants to know what's happening."

Rhys took the phone from his ear so he could speak to Toby, who was sitting on the couch waiting for a TV movie to start. "The police have been around the point near Brad's house. They set up huge spotlights in the bush. He went down to check it out." Then Rhys spoke into his mobile again. "Yeah, so what was going on? You're joking? Not those two again? What were they up to this time? Really? Yeah, tell me – then I'll tell Toby."

Rhys listened to Brad for several minutes. He knew that Toby was dying to hear what Brad was talking about.

"Yeah! Cool, we'll see you tomorrow." And he hung up. "This is whacked."

"What is?" asked Toby.

"Would either of you like some dessert while you watch the movie?" Mrs. Hampshire had an apple pie on a serving plate and was taking it over to the table.

"Not just yet, thanks, Mrs. H." Rhys would love some pie, but he'd had seconds of the spaghetti and meatballs. "Dinner was really great."

"Maybe later. Thanks, Mum." Toby was looking straight at Rhys, obviously more interested in Brad's phone call than in eating any dessert. "So it was drug smugglers, wasn't it? I was right, wasn't I? Come on, Rhys, what did Brad say?"

"Firstly, no, it wasn't." Rhys paused for dramatic effect. "Stuff wasn't being smuggled into the country – it *was* being smuggled *out*! But hang on, let me tell you what happened to Brad."

"What do you mean, what happened to Brad?" Toby was totally curious now.

"How can I tell you the story when you keep interrupting?" Rhys was having so much fun with this – he wanted to string it out for as long as he could. "Mrs. H, I *will* have some apple pie – just a small piece, if that's OK."

"Would you like whipped cream or ice cream with that, Rhys?" Mr. Hampshire was on his way to the table with a container of each.

"Um, can I have both, please?" asked Rhys.

"No problem." And while Toby's mum sliced

the pie, his dad scooped out some ice cream and then handed Rhys the whipped cream container and a spoon. "Go for it!"

"Rhys Morton, if you don't tell me every single thing Brad said, I'll …"

"You'll what, tough guy?" Rhys laughed and sat down on the other end of the couch, balancing his bowl of dessert. "OK, enough joking – here goes! But you'll probably miss the start of the movie – it's a long story."

"Obviously." Toby was getting impatient.

"Right. OK. So Brad saw police car lights flashing not far from his place and went down to investigate. Turns out the ridge walk was swarming with police and customs officers. They set up spots to make their search easier, but they actually found what they were after because – wait for it – Stacey and Jason told them where to look!"

"Go figure! So they're involved?"

"Not exactly. You know how we saw the twins tonight? Well, not long after that, they noticed some people tramping around in the bush near their place

– and so they went to have a closer look. Turns out there were two or three people acting suspiciously near Shiloh's boat shed."

"Yes! See, I said those people in the dinghy were heading for a boat shed!" Toby looked pretty pleased with himself.

"So, OK, do you want to know what happened? Stacey and Jason didn't get too close, but they could hear strange noises coming from inside the boat shed – and of course they knew it had been totally empty yesterday."

"You're kidding?" Toby was leaning so far forward that Rhys was afraid he'd fall off the couch. "What did the twins do? Did they find out what was inside?"

"No. They ran home, told their dad, then phoned the police. The police alerted Customs because they'd apparently had an anonymous tip - earlier today – and, by the time the authorities swarmed all over the area, those guys off the yacht were inside Shiloh's boat shed organizing a cachet of – you won't believe this – wild birds that had been delivered there sometime after we'd left yesterday. They're supposed to be worth big money on the overseas market."

Toby's parents had sat down in the family room, obviously interested in hearing the story too, so Rhys continued.

"Those guys were taking the birds out of cages, sedating them and stuffing them into PVC pipes, ready to transfer them to the boat. There were all sorts of birds: king parrots, red-tailed and yellow-tailed black cockatoos, Major Mitchell cockatoos, galahs and even rosellas."

"That's crazy." Toby was shaking his head. "Do you know how many of those birds would arrive alive? Hardly any. I researched bird smuggling for a debate last year – terrible. So the police grabbed the guys, right?"

"Yep, sure did, and they reckoned they couldn't have done it so quickly without the twins' help. Apparently, when he recognized their names, the sergeant didn't believe them at first – thought they were playing a joke on him. So their dad got on the phone and told the police he'd been down to check their story – and it was true – although at that stage none of them knew what was actually in the shed. Amazing, huh?"

"It sounds like that wildlife show you used to watch when you were little, doesn't it, Toby?" Mr. Hampshire seemed quite concerned. "Except this was for real."

"Those dreadful people." Mrs. Hampshire was really upset. "I had a galah when I was young. They're beautiful birds – I can't bear to think of them being smuggled overseas like that. It's so cruel."

"Yes, but thanks to Stacey and Jason, they're now safe with Customs and on their way to Quarantine. They'll be held there in cages as evidence, until those guys are charged and their accomplices caught – and then the birds will go back to the wild. Brad checked it out with the police."

"Thank goodness those kids did the right thing." Mrs. Hampshire was on her way to the kitchen. "Would anyone else like a cup of tea? I need one after hearing that dreadful story. Phillip?"

"Not for me, thanks, Rhonda." Mr. Hampshire looked at Rhys and then at Toby. "After that other business, I'm surprised that the twins did contact the police. Maybe they're not such bad kids after all. You never can tell, can you? It isn't wise to assume anything about anybody, is it?"

Rhys pursed his lips and tried to swallow his grin as he glared at Toby.

"But there is one assumption I think I can confidently make." Mr. Hampshire smiled at the boys. "And that's about the outcome of tomorrow's surfing competition! After what I've seen the last couple of days, I'm predicting that you guys will do really well in the Junior and Novice divisions. But I'm certainly not going to assume anything about the Veterans – I wouldn't dare to make a prediction about that one!"

"Well, I would!" Mrs. Hampshire had come back into the family room and was far more relaxed now, as she sat down with her cup of tea.

"From tomorrow's weather forecast, I predict it'll come down to the last man standing. When I was at the newsstand today, I heard a couple of locals say that it'll be good early tomorrow, but then we're in for strong offshore winds later in the afternoon – so the final heats might be tough!"

"Sounds like a challenge, gentlemen." Mr. Hampshire was laughing and practicing his surfing stance in the middle of the family room, his arms held straight out from his shoulders as though he were riding a wave. "Maybe we should all have an early night, so we're fighting fit to take on the elements tomorrow!"

"I'll pass, thanks, Dad. Even though the movie's already started, I'd like to watch it – it's got an amazing industrial tap scene, like in 'Tap Dogs,' featuring those two guys who gave our troupe some lessons last year. Remember – Chris and Steven? So I'd like to see it, although I probably won't watch the whole movie. You up for it, Rhys?"

"Sure. They're the dudes you told me about, aren't they?" Rhys remembered Toby saying what great tappers they were and how one day he hoped to get a professional gig with them. "Yeah, that'd be cool. Is that OK, Mr. H?"

"Absolutely," Toby's dad agreed. "Just don't stay up too late."

"Sure thing. Thanks, Dad. And Dad, I'm really looking forward to seeing you surf tomorrow."

"Good night, boys." Toby's mum smiled. "I hope your foot's feeling much better, Rhys."

"Yeah, thanks, Mrs. H – it's fine. Your frozen peas therapy did the trick! It's totally back to normal."

"Excellent. Well, enjoy the movie, guys." Toby's mother blew him a kiss. "See you for breakfast – I'll do eggs with everything."

And so Rhys and Toby were left to enjoy their movie, although before long Rhys realized that he couldn't concentrate on anything but the fact that tomorrow he'd be competing in his first Easter Surf. Tomorrow he could be – no, tomorrow he *would* be – the Junior Surfing Champion of Lorne. He had to be. He'd dreamed about nothing else since the first day he'd stood up on a board right here in Lorne.

Thirteen

"Check out those waves." Rhys was standing on the deck of the surf club, looking along the beach as the surf rolled in. "They're excellent. Three to six feet, hot and glassy."

"And that would mean?" Toby was such a kook – he still had so much to learn about surfing, but it was great that he was going to compete today.

Rhys was worried that the size of the waves might be a bit daunting for Toby, but, hey, he was in the Junior Novice section, so he had as much chance as any of the other contestants. Maybe more. For a beginner surfer he had such strong legs because he was a tapper – and that might just make the difference!

"OK, so the three-to-six feet bit means the height of the wave from the trough to the peak. It's good because some of them will be over your head, but not so big that it's dangerous." Rhys was confident those waves would help him win today.

"And *hot* means the wave stands up cleanly and runs away in one direction. See? Watch how they're forming. And they're called glassy because there's no wind and the water surface is perfect. Couldn't be better really."

"My heat is in half an hour." Toby sounded a bit anxious. "Can you remind me about all the stuff I've got to remember?"

"Sure. First up you check out the way the surf is breaking – that's what we've just been doing. OK, let's practice – we'll pick a wave from the next set and work out how you'd ride it. Look, see that one?" Rhys pointed at the third wave in the set and Toby nodded.

"See, if you chose that one you could ride it all the way to the beach and show the judges your stuff. But I might be better off waiting for a bigger one in the next set because then I could push my limits and that way I'd get more points."

"Right. Got it. Choose a wave that's best for me and makes me look good!" Toby laughed. "What else?"

"Yeah, that's it." Rhys looked at his watch. Not long now. "Keep checking behind you, and if you see a better wave coming, get off the one you're on and go for the next one. Remember, your ride isn't judged until your hands leave your board completely – so don't stand up until you're sure the wave you've chosen is a good one. It's kind of like when you're serving in tennis – if the ball isn't in the right spot, you don't hit it – you catch it and throw it up again. OK?"

"Yep. Got that, too." Toby was starting to look a lot more confident.

"You know the way this contest works – it's a knockout, so you'll be against one other guy in each heat, right? Just like when you and I share a wave, except this time you want to beat him." Rhys was sure Toby would be fine.

"So, first one on his feet, closest to the curl, is the guy in control of the wave – that gives you right-of-way, OK? You know how to do that. We've practiced it heaps. That's the way you'll win – by being a bit aggressive, taking control of the wave, but not interfering with the other surfer if he's on the same wave as you. And you can't drop in if someone's already on a wave. Easy."

"I'm starting to feel like I do before I tap in comps." Toby looked amazingly calm, focused and in control. "I'll give it my best shot – and maybe I'll even get a place. Who knows? I'm going out there to have fun. Mum always tells me to own the stage when I dance – maybe with the help of Dad's surfer genes I'll own the waves. Let's get down there, eh, coach?"

As they walked downstairs, Brad came running up two at a time, his skateboard under his arm. He turned around and went back down with them towards the marshaling area.

"Sorry I'm so late. I would have been here sooner, but it was my dad again. He drove down from the city early this morning so he could watch your dad compete today, Toby, but I had no idea he was coming. I'd left my skateboard out in the hall because Mum's cool since I took your advice and we talked about it the other afternoon. And she was going to talk to Dad, and ... but that's not important now because ..."

"Sorry, Brad, we don't have time – we're up soon." Rhys didn't want to be rude, but it was only ten minutes until the heats began. "It's cool you're here though, dude. Keep your fingers crossed for us."

The beach and shore were crowded with hundreds of people waiting for the Easter Surf to begin. If Rhys had been excited before, he was really high on adrenalin now. This was what he'd waited for – the chance to show off his skills in the surf – to prove to himself and everybody else that he had the potential to be a pro surfer.

A microphone crackled to life and interrupted Rhys's thoughts. "Ladies and gentlemen, boys and girls – and surfers!" Someone was trying to make himself heard, but it took the crowd a few minutes to realize that they needed to stop talking and listen.

"Toby, that guy's a legend." Rhys couldn't believe he was standing so close to one of the country's best-ever surfers. "His name's Alan, but they call him 'Huey' after the king of surfing! Cool name, huh? He's from Queensland."

Finally a hush fell over those people closest to the makeshift stage area in front of the surf club. Like most of the competitors, Rhys and Toby were on the sand, on the surf side of the stage.

"I'm Huey Johnston. I'm your MC for today. Welcome to the annual Easter Surf at Lorne. As most of you know, this competition for Juniors and Veterans was set up some years ago to coincide with the Bells Beach annual contest. We've got former Bells champions competing here today in the Veterans division – and even more exciting is that we reckon we've probably got future Bells champions here, too. They're going to show us their stuff in the Juniors."

Toby nudged Rhys with his elbow, nodded and grinned.

"So, the judges are ready, and the contestants are ready – let's not keep them waiting another second. It's going to be a long day, but a beauty, I can promise you that. So get out your beach chair or towel, settle back, and prepare to be amazed by the lineup of talent we have here today. Who knows what future stars we're about to discover. Enjoy the event, folks, and I'll catch up with you all right here for the presentations late this afternoon. Cheers!"

An ear-shattering hooter sounded over the loudspeaker system, announcing the start of the event.

"Good luck, boys." Toby's dad had managed to squeeze through the crowd on the beach. "*You can do it!"* Mr. Hampshire mimicked the voice Rhys often used.

"Seriously, I think you guys have a good chance. The waves are hot at the moment, so you'll have plenty of opportunity to show the judges what you can do. If Rhonda's right about the weather, and we get offshore winds this afternoon, the competition will really step up a notch. So, knock off as many as you can this morning, gentlemen – use this as your practice session! You'll need all the tricks you can pull out later on today!"

"Good advice – thanks, Mr. H." Rhys knew that if he was ever going to be a champion, today was the day. The surf was just right at the moment, with the promise of more challenging waves in the afternoon session, so he could really show them his stuff when the competition heated up.

"Yeah, thanks, Dad." Toby looked amazingly relaxed. "We'll meet you here just before your heat, so you can borrow Rhys's board, OK? That'll be great lunchtime entertainment."

"Fidget Hampshire versus Jellyfish O'Donnell."

Rhys liked the sound of that. He really wanted Toby's dad to win, of course, but he knew it could go either way and would be a great contest. "What legends!"

"I think there'll be more legends made today." Toby's dad looked confident about that. "Go for it, boys." And he slapped them both on the shoulder as they headed down to the water's edge to take part in their respective heats.

"Chookas!" Toby laughed. "Sorry, that's a dance thing."

"Good luck, dude!" Rhys had to focus. It was time to forget about everything but the waves. He was as ready as he'd ever be, so bring it on!

Fourteen

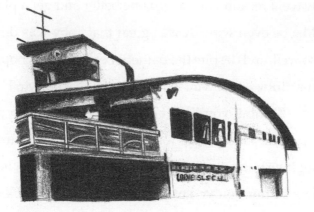

"So, who taught you to surf goofy-foot on a right-hand break, eh, kook?" Rhys had watched Toby's last ride and was amazed to see him put his right foot in front of his left. "And your flick off was really clean. No wonder you got the points. You looked awesome, dude. Like a champion! You must have a good teacher!"

"I'm stoked." Toby was breathing fast. "I'm in the final four, Rhys. Even if I don't beat the next guy, I'll at least get fourth. How cool is that?"

"Yeah, that's cool, but the way you rode that last wave, I reckon you can go one better and get a place. Maybe even win." It was great that Toby was doing so well, and despite the pathetic bet, Rhys was hoping that Toby *would* win. "What do you reckon, Mr. H?"

"I think you'll go close, Toby, if you keep that up." Mr. Hampshire looked very proud. "Third is looking good, but first isn't out of the question. For a late starter you've got fantastic style, and you seem to be intuitive when you're on a wave – a bit like your old man, huh? Speaking of which, wish me luck. It's time to see if I've still got what it takes – and if the knee surgery holds up." He picked up Rhys's board and tucked it under his arm. "Thanks for the loan, Rhys – I hope it does all that tricky stuff for me, too. You really shredded those waves in your heats – and you made a few of us old guys gasp when you pulled off that last one. Well done – just hope I can live up to your standards."

"Thanks, Mr. H. Good luck – find that wave with your name on it and make it yours!" Rhys was so high after his last wave that he almost felt as though everything around him was on a silent movie screen.

The noise, the crowd and the announcements over the speaker system – everything was sort of churning together and fading away somehow, so that it felt as if there were only the three of them on the beach: Rhys, Toby and his dad. It was like they were standing in a spotlight and everyone else had been put on pause. The whole thing felt surreal. He was on course to win the Junior Championship and so far the surf had given him just what he wanted. Hopefully the weather would work in his favor.

"There's Jason." Toby's words jolted Rhys back from wherever he'd been. Toby nodded towards the water's edge. "I didn't think he'd dare to compete after what's happened. How'd he do this morning, do you know?"

"He won all his heats easily." Rhys hadn't been expecting Jason to compete either. "He's a pretty aggressive surfer. I'll be up against him sometime after lunch for sure. But, get this – Stacey's in the finals, too. I reckon she's even better than her brother. I wonder whose boards they're using? Hey, the Veterans heats are starting. We can't miss this."

Rhys and Toby found a good spot on the stone wall and waited for the contest to begin.

"You guys were awesome this morning." Brad plonked himself down beside them. "So, you're both through to this afternoon, aren't you? That's excellent. How's your dad doing, Toby? Is he winning, too? I went to the skate park for a bit. I haven't missed him, have I?"

"No. It's just about to start." Toby looked behind Brad. "So your dad didn't come after all? Didn't you say he was here?"

"Yeah, but I didn't want him hanging out with me, so I told him he'd get a better view from the surf club." Brad indicated the deck behind them. "There he is – see? And Mum's here, too, with your mum. They don't know anything about surfing, but they both wanted to be here for your dad. Is he any good?

Do you think he'll do OK?"

"Take a look for yourself, dude." Rhys pointed and was pleased to see Mr. Hampshire pick the right wave out of a fairly uneven set. "He's an awesome surfer – the other guy has no chance, no chance at all. We can check this heat off – he's got it in the bag. Who wants some lunch? I'll go upstairs and grab it."

"I'm fine." Brad was sitting there spinning the wheels on his skateboard.

"That'd be great. Thanks." Toby answered without taking his eyes off the surf. "He's good, isn't he?"

"Yeah, he's good all right – good enough to take the Veterans title, I reckon." Rhys wanted to get the lunch quickly so he didn't miss anything. "Right, so you want chocolate milk and a chicken sandwich?"

"Sure. Chocolate milk and a sandwich. Yeah, great." Toby spoke like an automated toy. "I had no idea he was *that* good – he really could take this out, Rhys, couldn't he? How amazing is that?"

"Ah, not at all!" Rhys smiled at Toby, who

looked quite stunned, not unlike the old rabbit caught in the car headlights. "Your dad's a surfing legend, dude – just because he hadn't surfed for ages until this week doesn't mean he can't cut it. He can, and I want to be back with lunch before his next ride, so I'm out of here. Talk among yourselves till I get back – and keep my spot. It's getting crowded!"

Rhys sprinted up the stairs of the surf club, but because he was in such a hurry, he didn't notice that someone was standing at the top, until he'd crashed into them.

"What the ..." Rhys was stunned, but he managed to catch a carton of chips, loaded with ketchup, that threatened to land on top of him.

"You late for the bus or something, dude?" It was Stacey, with Jason not far behind her. "It leaves from outside the bank. If you hurry, you'll still make it. No point hanging around here and getting thumped, although I saw you competing; you're not bad – for a boy!" She giggled meanly, and then kept on talking. "Jason and I are up against each other in the next round, so I reckon it'll be one of us versus you in the final heat. Those boards we got hold of aren't too flash, but we're so good we'll beat you anyway. What do you reckon, Jase?"

Outside there was a roar from the crowd.

"You got no hope, dude." Jason sniggered at Rhys and continued down the stairs. "You and me in the final shootout, bro!" And he snorted with laughter, as his teeth ripped into his lunch.

"He wishes!" Stacey just sneered at her brother's back, then, grinning broadly, she snatched her bucket of chips away from Rhys and left without saying another word.

"Yeah – whatever!" Rhys raised his eyebrows in disbelief. Those two were a real worry, but he had to forget about them and focus on his own performance this afternoon. Meanwhile, lunch. He grabbed what he needed from the competitors' buffet and raced back down to the stone wall.

"You missed Dad's ride." Toby sounded disappointed. "He did this … I don't know what it's called. It looked awesome."

"I heard someone call it a quasimoto." Brad

looked impressed. "An older dude said he hadn't seen anyone pull it off so well in years. Mr. Hampshire was crouched down with his back flat and the wave kind of curled over the top of him. He looked like a pro doing an ad for Quiksilver or something. It was amazing. Everybody cheered."

"I wondered what the noise was! That's sure to clinch it for him." Rhys was certain about that. "Knew that board of mine was a winner! I'm sorry I missed it, but I ran into Stacey and Jason in the club. Literally." Rhys handed Toby his lunch. "They're so competitive, even against each other. Don't know what their problem is, but if I'm going to win this, I'm sure to be up against one of them in the final round. Just hope they don't get too aggro out there – they're bad enough on dry land!"

"Wouldn't put it past them to try something tricky." Toby took a bite of his lunch. "But we'll know soon enough."

Fifteen

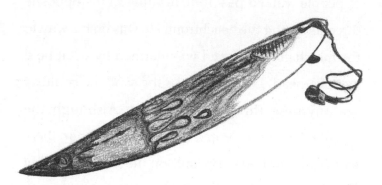

Rhys wasn't surprised that the predicted off shore winds were doing a mammoth job taking the chop out of the waves and holding them up for much longer, so that the rides were far steeper than they had been earlier in the day. It was lucky that the Novice and Veteran sections had finished. Rhys doubted any of those competitors would have dared to go out in this swell.

"A big tree's down – someone's been hit – the ambulance is there – looks pretty bad – over in the park – up behind the surf club."

Rhys couldn't make out all the details as a group of people walked past him, heading in the opposite direction along the beachfront. He was on his way to the marshaling area and was alarmed by what he'd just overhead. Looking across the sand, he couldn't see anything through the crowd. Although the weather had deteriorated during the last hour, there were still hundreds of people on the shore watching the wrap-up of the Easter Surf.

Rhys hadn't seen Toby since his friend's last ride, but he was sure Toby wouldn't have had any reason to be in the park. But it could be Brad. Hang on – how come Brad had his board with him today when his father was around? He'd even said he'd been to the skate park. It didn't make sense, but there was no time to work that out now.

Anyway, Brad and Toby would be hanging out at the surf club together, watching the final rounds of the Junior competition. Rhys was sure that neither of his friends would have been anywhere near that fallen tree. He hoped not, anyway. Yes, he was positive – it wasn't Toby or Brad.

Strange about those old trees though – who'd be stupid enough to walk underneath them in this wind? They'd been there forever, and whenever there were strong winds, they swayed threateningly. Rhys wasn't at all surprised to hear that one had finally snapped and fallen over.

"Rhys, your ride was sensational!" It was Toby. See, he was fine – and so was Brad who was just a few steps behind him.

"You're in the final two – that's awesome." Brad seemed really pleased for him.

"Yeah, you were brilliant." Toby's cheeks were flushed.

"My dad videoed the whole thing." Brad was really pumped. "We can watch it later. You were excellent, and now you've just got that chick to beat – should be easy."

"Thanks, I'm glad you guys are so confident." Rhys was feeling anything but confident. "After watching Stacey trounce Jason, I know she's going to be hard to beat. He pulled out everything he could, but nothing worked – not even trying to force her off that wave when he got aggro. She's the best Junior I've seen – ever! Seriously, she's got amazing style, technique *and* strength – she deserves to win the championship. And this wind is going to make it even harder. There'd be a lot of surfers who wouldn't dare to go out in that."

Rhys had a quick glance out the back. "The waves are really steep now. If the wind gets much stronger, it might be a blowout – they could stop the comp. I hope that doesn't happen – I want to surf the final round. How'd you do, Toby? I'm sorry our last heats were on at the same time."

"You mean you don't know?" Brad put the back of his hand to his forehead and play-acted major shock.

"Well?" Rhys looked at Toby whose face was blank, while his cheeks were still red. Was he sad or happy? "Tell me. Quick. I've got to get out there for the final. Did you get a place?"

"Did he get a place?" Brad nodded his head. "Yes, he got a place – second place!"

"How cool is that, Rhys?" Toby didn't seem to be able to say anything else. He was grinning like a smiley.

"That's brilliant, Tobes. Congratulations." Rhys kept looking over his shoulder, checking out the waves. He only had a couple more minutes before he had to be back in the surf. "I knew you'd do well. And what about your dad? How did he do? Was he OK on your board?"

But his voice was drowned out by the hooter, which announced the start of the Juniors' final round.

"Sorry. Tell me later. Hey, did you hear about a tree falling on someone? Check it out. Gotta go. Wish me luck – I'll need it." And he raced along the shore towards the marshaling area.

Stacey was already there, stamping her feet in the sand. "What do you mean?" she screamed at the marshal. "Of course we're going out – that surf's not too big. I've been out in worse than that heaps of times."

"Is there a problem?" Rhys was hardly game to ask because it looked like Stacey was the problem.

"They're thinking about canceling the final because they reckon it's too rough."

Rhys squinted into the wind. "It is pretty huge."

Stacey was scowling and thumping the flat of one hand against her board. "Aren't you game to go out in the big waves? Is that the problem? Go on, I dare you – then I can beat the pants off you, like I slaughtered Jason. And I'll be the champion. As if I'm not already."

"That surf's not a problem." Rhys hoped he sounded confident. The swell had certainly increased in the last ten minutes, but it wasn't what he considered dangerous. "I'm game, but I guess it's not up to us. The club will make that decision."

The wind was whipping around them, throwing sand into people's faces and making it very difficult to see or hear what was going on. Rhys tried to work out what was happening.

There were a couple of people, including Huey Johnston, up on the club's deck. They had binoculars and were checking out the surf, obviously making a decision about whether to cancel the final round or not.

Rhys backed away from Stacey and focused on the surf. He couldn't afford to be distracted by her antics – it was probably all part of a plan to unsettle him, so she'd have the advantage if they did finally get to surf. He'd seen that sort of psychology used before.

He checked the surf again. The swell had really increased, but it was still OK. He'd ridden this sort of break plenty of times – it was tricky, but, if they were allowed to complete the round, it would definitely sort out the winner.

"Could the contestants come forward, please?" It was Huey Johnston. "The committee has made a decision, and if you'd prefer, we're quite happy to delay the final heat until tomorrow. We don't think the conditions are dangerous, but they are quite challenging. So it's up to the two of you – you decide. If one of you wants to delay it, then we'll hold it tomorrow. What do you think?"

Well, that was a fair offer, but Rhys was happy to surf today – if he couldn't surf well in these conditions and win, then he didn't deserve to be awarded the championship, did he? And if Stacey surfed the swell better than him, then she deserved to be the winner. Simple.

"I'm good," he said.

"So am I." Stacey seemed very determined. She'd already picked up her board and was heading towards the water.

"Wait up!" Huey Johnston called after her.

"What?" Stacey flounced around and glared at Huey.

"There's just one condition: If you surf today, you get one ride each – that's it." Huey Johnston stood with his hands on his hips, an inflexible look on his face. "We can't risk the swell getting out of hand. So, you both get one crack at it. OK? You'll be judged on that one wave and we'll award the championship accordingly. It's harsh, but we reckon it's fair under the circumstances."

"Whatever! I only need one wave to prove that I'm the best!" Stacey swung around again, and strode off towards the surf.

"That's fine with me." Rhys was impatient to get into the water, too. He wanted the chance to win the title right now, today.

As he waded in, then fought his way through the strong waves, Rhys realized that he hadn't seen Jason since the twins had competed against each other, maybe fifteen or twenty minutes ago. He certainly hadn't been on the beach just now.

Strange. Rhys thought Jason should be there cheering for his sister. Those two behaved very differently from the way Rhys had always imagined twins would react to each other. They definitely had a weird relationship.

But there was no time to think about any of that now, either. There was just one thing he had to concentrate on. He had to get out the back and find the wave that would make him the champion.

Sixteen

With the water swirling around him, Rhys sat on his board and tried to keep his excitement under control. This had to be the ride of his life – this *would* be the ride of his life.

He had one chance at this championship. He had to take his time and choose just the right wave. Patience, Rhys, patience. Remember, if you pick one and it's not right, get off it. There'll be a better one. There's always a better one.

Adrenalin was ringing in his ears. His breath was short. Everything depended on his choice of wave. Take your time, Rhys. Take your time. There's no rush. Look, there's Stacey – she's not rushing. One wave, Rhys. One wave. Let this one go. And the next one. They're not good enough to win on. No rush. There's no rush.

The swell was huge now. The offshore wind was creating some amazing waves. If there wasn't so much at stake, Rhys knew he'd be jumping on any one of them and enjoying some of the best surfing ever.

And then it was there, behind him, rising with the promise of being the perfect wave. It was the second wave of the set, so he could coast on the swell of the first and be in the right position as it came to him. Rhys paddled as hard as he could, knowing he needed to be traveling as fast as the powerful wave when it arrived and lifted him up.

Taking no risks, Rhys gave one last strong stroke and he was on it, making sure that he kept the board flat on the water. He centered his weight and prepared to stand up. He landed on the balls of his feet, knees bent. Quickly he moved his left foot down the board and placed his right foot behind him, across the board. He was in exactly the position to make this work for him.

Rhys was facing the wave. It was peaking right. It was hot. It had a clean face, with nice big walls. He had chosen the ideal wave. Traveling sideways along it, he knew he had to rip it up and prove to the judges once and for all that he was the champion.

It was the best ride ever and it seemed to go on and on. Rhys leaned back, dropped down the wave, bottom-turned and whacked the lip. He'd shredded it. Surfing didn't get much better than this. He'd done it – he was sure it was the championship ride. Water sprayed in his face and he felt elated.

When he finally remembered to breathe again, Rhys also remembered something else: Stacey. The championship wasn't his yet. It all depended on Stacey.

Rhys turned around and looked out the back.

He wondered whether Stacey had gotten her ride yet. At first he couldn't see over the huge swell, so he walked up the beach a bit to get a good look at what she was doing. Yes, there she was on an absolutely superb wave, surfing it backhand, heels close to the inside rail, ripping it up and looking like a champion. She was *so* good.

Had his ride been better than hers? Right now, on the beach watching Stacey, Rhys wasn't sure. His had felt like the ultimate ride, but how did it look to the judges? How did it compare to Stacey's? She was such a brilliant surfer – there was no way he'd win. She was awesome. He was sure she was the champion.

But then, as Stacey dropped down the wave, things changed in a split second. Rhys couldn't believe it. For some reason, as Stacey bottom-turned, she hit the lip too late. Rhys sucked in his breath and held it. The wave had broken too much and it pushed Stacey back so that she got smacked. Her ride was over. Her championship hopes were ruined. She'd been hammered.

Stacey disappeared into the wave as her board flipped up in the air. It was one gnarly wipeout!

"You've won, Rhys! You've won!" Toby appeared from nowhere and tackled Rhys to the sand. "You're the Lorne Easter Surf Junior Champion. Your ride was amazing. Blew me away. Congratulations, you're the champion!"

"You're the champion!" Brad sounded like an echo, as he jumped on top of them, laughing and hollering like a madman. "Champion! Champion! Champion! Woohoo!"

"Congratulations, Rhys!" It was Toby's dad, whirling a towel in the air to celebrate the victory. Toby's mum was there, too. So were Mr. and Mrs. Lynch.

Rhys, Toby and Brad pulled each other to their feet.

"That was a really brilliant display, young man." Even standing on the beach in a howling wind, Mrs. Lynch seemed very formal. "Congratulations. Braddon is so fortunate to have such talented friends – a first and a second. We'll have to organize a special celebration tonight."

"Absolutely!" Mr. Lynch was still using his video camera. "What a day. The three of you are champions as far as I'm concerned! Sue's right – we'll have to work out a really special treat to mark the occasion."

"Do you mean you placed, too, Mr. H?" Rhys hadn't quite come to terms with his own success yet because he had been sure Stacey had nailed it until her unexpected wipeout.

"Yes, Rhys, Phillip – I mean Fidget – won the Veterans." Mrs. Hampshire laughed and smiled proudly. "But, just as I predicted, it was last man standing."

"What do you mean?" Rhys picked up his board and they all started walking up the beach towards the surf club, with Toby and Brad mucking around beside him, like a couple of playful puppies.

"Well, it was a battle royal, as they say." Mr. Hampshire took Rhys's board from him. "Let me take that, champ. You must be worn out after that sensational ride."

"Thanks." Rhys just grinned as the reality began to sink in. He was the Junior Champion. "But tell me – what happened?"

"You won't believe it." Toby pushed Brad, and Brad pushed him back. Both of them laughed hysterically. "It was just like in the movies. You tell him, Dad."

"OK. The brief version." Mr. Hampshire leaned Rhys's surfboard against the makeshift stage where the presentations would soon be held. "Jellyfish and I were the last two, so we were all set for the final shootout, as he called it. I don't mind admitting I was a bit worried about using Toby's board." He smiled at his wife. "Anyway, in the end it didn't matter. We were heading out for the final heat, but, being the crazy that he is from way back, Jellyfish insisted we walk over the rocks and go into the surf from there to save time and energy, and …"

"And he stepped on a sea urchin." Brad laughed loudly. "And he got so many spines stuck in his foot that he couldn't surf the final heat. Can you believe that? It's dumb, but true."

"So Dad didn't even have to surf again." Toby was obviously trying to be polite and not laugh. He was so proud of his father.

"Last man standing!" Mr. Hampshire smiled at Rhys. "The champion by default. That's me. And, to tell you the truth, I wasn't sorry I didn't have to go out in that swell. It's a long time since I took on waves that size. But you – you shredded it, boyo. Bells, look out – Rhys Morton is heading your way sometime soon."

The loudspeaker crackled once again. "Ladies and gentlemen, would you gather around, please." Huey Johnston was at the microphone. "We'll be presenting the championship trophies in about five minutes, so if you need to do anything else first, like put on your makeup, be quick!" The crowd guffawed at his joke.

"Did anyone see Stacey leave the water?" Rhys was suddenly aware that he'd completely forgotten about his rival. "Is she OK?"

"Of course I'm OK." Stacey was standing right behind him. "You don't think a piddling wave like that could hurt me, do you? Should have nailed it. Anyway, there's always next year. Good ride, Rhys." And then she walked away towards the girls' changing rooms.

"Thanks." She'd left so quickly that Rhys doubted she'd even heard him. He was surprised by what she'd said – it had almost sounded as though they were friends.

"Ladies and gentlemen, before the presentation begins, regrettably there's a brief announcement we have to make. As some of you may know, a tree came down in the park this afternoon and a local was injured on his way to the beach. It was bad luck, to say the least, but you'll be pleased to know that his injuries weren't severe."

He paused for a moment and then continued. "And does anyone know where Stacey Fletcher went after that final heat in the Juniors? Unfortunately, she's needed at the hospital. We've got someone on standby to drive her there, so if you do know where she is, please send her over to the stage immediately."

Rhys looked at Toby. Toby shrugged.

"Did you find out anything about the accident?" Rhys suddenly felt sick. "Was Jason the one under the tree? Is that what Huey means?" It was bad enough that someone had been hurt, but the prospect of its being someone he knew made it seem even worse.

But before Toby answered, Stacey came running out of the club straight towards them.

"Where's Jason? Jase, where are you? What Huey said – does that mean ..." And then she fainted, lurching forward without warning and falling heavily onto the sand before anyone had a chance to catch her.

"Go figure!" said Toby.

Seventeen

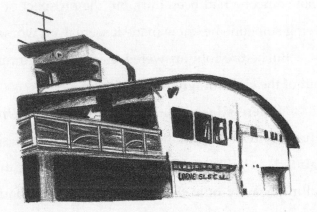

"So what was that about?" Brad looked worried. "Is Stacey OK?"

"Yeah. There was a bit of a mix-up. Stacey thought Jason had been hit by the tree, but it was their dad." Being the closest to Stacey when she fell, Rhys had taken control of the situation, and with Toby lending a hand, he'd sorted things out.

"Once she felt OK, we helped her to the car that was waiting to drive her to the hospital. Turns out Mr. Fletcher only has a broken arm. Jason was already there – he went straight up after he lost to Stacey. He didn't want her to know about their dad's accident until she'd surfed the final heat. Thoughtful, huh?"

"I don't get it." Toby shook his head and shrugged. "Those two have a totally weird relationship, don't they? Even my big sister and I get along better than they do most of the time – and they're twins. What do you reckon their problem is?"

"Ladies and gentlemen, it's finally time for our presentations." Huey Johnston was back at the microphone, so Rhys had no chance to let Toby know what Stacey had told him just before she'd left for the hospital. He'd have to save that for later.

"Sorry for the delay," Huey continued. "Couldn't be helped. Anyway, everything's shipshape now, so it's trophy time."

Rhys didn't really hear much of what was said after that because, now that the Stacey thing had been sorted out, he was floating in some incredible place where he could at last focus on his win. He was the Junior Champion. He let the feeling wash over him like the awesome wave that had made it possible.

He'd phone his parents as soon as he could. He didn't have his mobile with him – he'd left it at the resort as he always did when he went surfing. Shouldn't be too long now, though.

Mr. Hampshire had already been up on stage to get his trophy and his twin-tail, which Rhys hoped to try out sometime soon. And Toby had been up, too, although Rhys hadn't really been listening to everything that had been said. He was too self-absorbed. He was the champion.

"Did you hear that, Rhys?" Toby was standing next to him now, clutching his gift certificate and his trophy for coming second in the Novice section. "Huey called me *Midget* Hampshire! How cool is that! Dad's stoked."

"That's excellent. Every surfer needs a nickname! That's perfect. Midget. Yeah, that's really cool." Rhys was struggling to tune in to what was happening around him. It was all a bit of a blur, but he was really pleased that both Toby and his dad had done so well in their sections. And he liked the nickname thing: Midget, son of Fidget. Yeah, that worked.

"And the winner of our Junior section is a dark horse, Rhys *Rambo* Morton. Where have you been all this time, Rambo? You're obviously a well-kept secret! Those of us who come from out of state had never heard of you until you shredded the surf today. Come up on stage, young fella, so I can have the honor of shaking your hand. Ladies and gentlemen, please congratulate our Junior Surf Champion, Rhys Rambo Morton."

"What the ..." Rhys was confused. "Where did that come from? I don't have a nickname." He looked at Toby for help.

"You do now! Hey, it's from your initials: RAM – Rhys Alexander Morton. Perfect!" Toby thumped him on the back and pointed him in the direction of the stairs that led up onto the stage.

Rhys felt as though his feet were floating a

few inches above the ground as the crowd, who were clapping and cheering, seemed to propel him forward without the need to walk. It definitely felt like being in a dream. He had no control over what he was doing – it was all just happening to him.

"Congratulations on your win today, Rambo." Huey Johnston held up his hand to quiet the crowd. "You seriously blew us away! And I have no hesitation in saying that in years to come, you'll be holding up the Bells Beach trophy."

The crowd erupted, shouting their agreement. Rhys was feeling totally out of control. This was surreal. Until now he was sure he'd only won because Stacey had wiped out, but from what Huey was saying, that wasn't true. He'd won because he was the best.

"Thanks, Mr. Johnston. Thanks so much." It was all Rhys could manage as he shook hands with this surfing legend. He felt overwhelmed as he held the winner's trophy above his head. Huey Johnston was a surfer Rhys had admired forever and here he was telling everyone that Rhys would be a Bells champion one day. Go figure!

"Now you all know about the prizes for this championship – the trophy and the gift certificate, donated by Jellyfish's surf shop." Huey Johnston had a twinkle in his eyes, but Rhys had no idea what he was going to say next.

"What you don't know is that I've been approached only moments ago by a representative from Quiksilver, and based on Rambo's performance today, they're offering him a full sponsorship endorsement for a minimum of three years. You might have noticed Rambo sealed his victory on a Quiksilver board."

Rhys hugged the trophy to his chest and tried to make sense of what Mr. Johnston was saying.

"That means, folks, that whatever surfing event Rambo wants to compete in, no matter where it is in Australia, Quiksilver will supply him with clothes and equipment, fly him to the event and pay for all his expenses while he's there."

Huey Johnston held up his hand to silence the crowd. "That's how confident we all are that this young fella will become an Australian surfing champion in the next few years – before he travels overseas and represents us in the World Championship! Congratulations, Rambo. You're an outstanding champion – in fact, I'll put my reputation on the line here and say that you're the most talented Junior Champion I've seen in years!"

The crowd cheered again and then people came from everywhere, rushing up onto the stage and surrounding Rhys. Toby and the Hampshires, plus Brad and the Lynches, were there, as well as heaps of people he'd never even met. Everyone seemed to want to hug him or kiss him or slap him on the back. Everyone seemed as excited as he was, if that were possible.

"Three cheers for Rambo!" Toby and Brad yelled together. And the crowd erupted once again, whooping and hollering like a stadium full of crazy soccer fans. People called his name and cameras clicked.

Eventually the crowd began to dwindle and the noise died down. There were only a few people left on the stage now. Rhys felt Toby take hold of his elbow, leading him off the platform and down the stairs. Rhys had no idea where they were going, but it didn't really matter.

"Here. Have a drink and get your breath, Rhys." Mr. Hampshire handed him a can of something and settled him on the wall in front of the surf club. "We're so proud of you, mate. Your parents will be, too. Why don't you use my phone and give them a call now."

Rhys took the mobile and tried to dial his home number, but the digits all seemed to swim together and not make any sense. He handed the phone to Toby. "It's too tricky." He laughed, feeling weird that he couldn't even remember his own phone number. "Can you dial it for me?"

Rhys heard the ping of the numbers being keyed in and then Toby gave him back the phone. His dad was telling him to hang on while his mum picked up the other extension – they both wanted to hear what he had to say.

"I'm the Junior Champion. And I've got a

sponsorship from Quiksilver. How cool is that? Yeah, all my expenses for three years." He knew his mum was crying and his dad was obviously shocked. "I'll call you later when we're back at the resort. OK? Yeah, me, too." Rhys felt his eyes start to water, and brushing his hand over his face as though his hair were in his eyes, he handed the mobile back to Toby.

"Well, what did they say?" Toby was sitting on the wall next to him.

"Mum said she wished she could have been here to see me. She said she'll be here next year for sure. Dad was so blown away – he said he knew I was good, but not *that* good. He joked that he wanted to take out a full-page ad in the newspaper to make sure everyone knew that his son was a champion surfer!"

"We can save him the trouble." There were several people Rhys somehow hadn't noticed,who were standing right in front of him. "I'm Rohan Andrews from Channel 8 and this is Kane Sackett, a reporter from The Standard. We'd like to interview you now if that's OK, so we can add it to our footage of your winning ride and get it back to the city for tonight's sports report. Kane needs to write the story for tomorrow's early edition. How do you feel about that?"

Rhys looked at Toby, who grinned back and nodded his head enthusiastically.

"Rhys would love to do an interview." Mr. Hampshire had answered for him, which was lucky because, after the conversation with his parents, Rhys was finding it hard to talk. "Just give him five minutes to get his head together, guys, OK? This is all a bit overwhelming, as you can imagine. Meanwhile, my son and I will be happy to fill you in on any basic details for the newspaper, if that's a help. Rhys, why don't you have a quick shower first. That should clear the cobwebs."

So, without totally taking off his wetsuit, Rhys stood for several minutes under the warm shower in the surf club, letting the soothing water flow over his hair, face, shoulders and back, until he felt ready to talk to the reporter and television crew.

"Here – Mrs. Hampshire thought you might need this." Brad handed him a towel. Rhys dried off his hair and pushed it back off his face.

"Thanks. How unreal is this, Brad?" Rhys dropped the towel, not really thinking about what he was doing. He noticed that Brad picked it up and together they walked outside to where the guys were waiting to do the interview.

"Yep, it doesn't get much better than this." Brad laughed. It felt as though they'd been friends for a long time. "Champ, your public awaits you! *You can do it!*"

Eighteen

"Now *this* is a sleepover!" Rhys couldn't believe what Mr. Lynch had organized for the three of them. "When your parents said we should have a sleepover I was like, yeah, right, we had those when we were little. But our own room at the Cumberland for one night, with as much room service as we can eat, plus continuous on-demand movies – after we've watched my interview, of course! I'm dreaming, right?"

"Nope. It's true." Brad passed Rhys the huge plate of chips and a smaller one of mayonnaise. Their super-deluxe hamburgers had been delicious.

"This was Dad's idea." Brad put another chip into his mouth. "Mum's stuck on throwing you a party at our place tomorrow – she loves doing stuff like that. She'll spend all night planning it! She used to be an event coordinator – that's how she met Dad – but she stopped working when they got married. Because she's got so much free time they have people for dinner a lot. But what she loves most is giving mega parties, so she's always looking for an excuse – and this time you're it!"

Rhys noticed that Toby looked at him with an I-told-you-so stare, so he gave him a right-back-at-you grin.

"Anyway, my dad said you'd had such a huge day that you both needed a quiet time tonight, so he managed to get this room for us. How mad is it, having our own place, even though it is next door to the Hampshires'?"

"Yeah, it's totally cool." Toby seemed as puzzled as Rhys felt. "Especially since my sister and her friend have arrived a day early. But how come your dad was so generous, Brad? I mean, sure he's Dad's boss, but he hardly knows Rhys and me."

Brad seemed to be working out his answer. Rhys wouldn't have dared to ask Brad why his father had gotten the room for them, but he was sure Toby was right – there had to be more to this than they'd been told so far.

"I think Dad felt awkward about the skateboard stuff." Without explaining what he meant, Brad got up and walked out onto the balcony. Rhys followed Brad outside and stood next to him at the railing. Toby joined them.

"What's up?" Instead of looking at his new friend, Rhys stared out at the ocean.

"I tried to tell you this morning, remember? Before your first heat."

"Go on." Rhys was sure now that Mr. Lynch's generosity wasn't just because of their combined success in the surf today.

"OK. Here goes. Last year when he was driving to work in the city one morning, Dad saw a teenager knocked off his skateboard by a car. Dad stopped to help, but the skater died before the ambulance arrived." Brad took a big breath. "Dad was devastated. Apparently he kept seeing it like a video replay and thinking it could have been me. But he didn't say anything to Mum or me – he just kept it inside, and suddenly refused to let me skate anymore. He just gave lame excuses all the time. It's been so difficult between us for months now because it didn't make sense – one day I was allowed to skate, next day I wasn't. He and Mum seemed to stop talking to each other. If only he'd told us."

Rhys and Toby just listened. There was nothing to say.

"When he saw my skateboard in the hall today, he absolutely lost it. At first he screamed stupid stuff like I was grounded for the rest of my life, but before Mum could calm him down and talk about it, he'd slumped down into a chair and started crying. It was awful. My dad was crying. I'd never seen him cry."

Brad stopped again as a skateboarder rolled past on the street below the resort.

"That's when he told us about the skater. Mum said he should have shared it with us when it happened – that it would have helped him with the grief and stuff. But you know how it is – he runs a stockbroking firm – he's supposed to be macho, able to handle any situation." There was another pause. This was a really tough call."But he couldn't – he got cranky instead. It was like he totally changed – and he pushed us both away. Now it all kind of makes sense, because he's finally told us. Mum reckons it's going to take a long time for him to get over it."

"Wow." Rhys let out the breath he'd been holding. "That's some story. Imagine keeping that to yourself. It's nightmare stuff. No wonder he didn't want you to skate."

"Yeah. Anyway, we've got a deal now – I promised I'll only ride in parks – he's cool with that." Brad smiled happily. "And he's encouraging Mum to go for a catering job at the transportation planning firm where your mum works, Toby – it'd be part-time. My dad thinks it'd suit her really well." The boys grinned at each other.

Brad looked excited. "But wait for it – Dad wants his firm to sponsor a skating competition here in Lorne, starting next summer. He's going to talk to Jellyfish about it this week so they can get it organized. Cool, huh?"

"Excellent!" Rhys did the calculations in his head. "That gives us eight months to practice. Tomorrow Toby and I will use our gift certificates to get our boards from Jellyfish's shop. Hey, now I get it – that's why you had your board with you today. This is so cool."

"Can you show me how to skate, too, Brad?" Toby seemed pretty keen. "I reckon it looks amazing. You'll have to teach me some of those gnarly tricks so I can beat the twins next summer! They're sure to enter."

"No worries!" laughed Brad. And then the doorbell rang.

Nineteen

"Guess it's room service. That was quick." Rhys was surprised – they'd only ordered their dessert a few minutes before.

"Hey, Toby." But it wasn't a waiter; it was Toby's sister.

"What's up, Carolyn?"

"I just remembered that you got a phone call at

home this week. I was going to text you, but the guy said it wasn't urgent. You can call him when you get back. But Dad said to tell you now."

"Tell me what?" Toby looked blank.

"OK, I wrote it down." Carolyn took a scrunched-up piece of paper out of her jeans. "Fashion Week. Industrial. Ten tappers. Phone Chris."

Toby just stared at his sister. Rhys stood behind him wondering what she was talking about.

"Which means?" Toby didn't seem to understand what Carolyn was on about either.

"You can be so thick sometimes, Toby Hampshire." Carolyn stuck the note out in front of her brother and shrugged. "You've got a gig. You're doing a tap routine with that guy Chris – and you're going to be paid for it, dork. His mobile number is there. Call him."

And she walked away towards their parents' place next door. "What a waste of a perfectly good room." And then the door slammed behind her, echoing hollowly on the quarry-tiled landing.

Rhys stood in the hallway of the boys' room and waited for Toby to react. It didn't take long.

"Are you serious? I've got a professional gig. I'm going to be paid to tap. Yes! It's Chris – the guy we saw in the movie last night. Yes, yes, yes!" Toby started doing a tap routine in bare feet on the carpet.

Then the doorbell rang again – and this time it was room service with their dessert: three of the biggest chocolate ice cream sundaes ever.

"These are so huge." Rhys was amazed. "I can't believe they actually stayed in these glass bowls – it's like they're about to surf out onto the tray."

As they sat around the dining table eating their dessert, Rhys thought it might be a good time to tell Toby and Brad what he'd found out about the twins.

"You know you were wondering about Stacey and Jason?"

They just nodded, their mouths packed with sundae.

"While we were sitting in the surf club, before

Stacey left for the hospital, she told me a whole lot of stuff. Her dad's a single parent. Her mother died when the twins had just started school. She was working on the fishing boat and there was an accident. Stacey didn't go into that."

Rhys thought how much he'd miss his own mum if she died, even though things had been strained between them until recently.

"Stacey said that since then her dad has been seriously overprotective – he doesn't want her to do the things that Jason does. That's why he let Jason sell her stuff. She's always tried to prove that she's just as good as her brother, and in the end she became obsessed with being better than him at everything – even stealing." Rhys stopped to have a drink. "She said she'd proved her point in the surf today. But when she thought Jason had been hurt, she was totally shocked – and she says she won't be doing any of that dumb stuff anymore."

No one spoke. They ate their sundaes in silence, until Rhys continued his story.

"And she said the police have put them on a

good-behavior bond because of how they helped solve the attempted bird smuggling. They have to do some community service, too – help out at the surf club, teaching the little kids and cleaning up the surf boats and stuff. She actually seemed pretty excited about that."

"That's good." Toby swallowed a mouthful. "Sounds like it's been pretty hard for them – she's not as feral as she makes out, is she? I'd guessed it was a bit of an act. Tough chicks don't faint."

"But she's a great surfer, isn't she?" Brad looked straight at Rhys. "She's the runner-up Junior Champion, which is huge. And Jason got third – that's good, too. So how did she think her dad would take that news?"

"She wasn't sure." Rhys thought about it. "But I think he should be pleased because, even though Stacey doesn't know yet, Mr. Johnston told me that she's got herself a one-year Roxy sponsorship. And Jason's won a limited endorsement, too, so long as he stays out of trouble with the police. How good is that?"

"That's excellent." Toby seemed genuinely pleased. "Let's hope it stops them both helping themselves to other people's things."

"But they're so competitive." Brad made a face to indicate that he was unimpressed. "Do you think that'll change now?"

"I'm not sure. I mean, maybe that's just how they are." Rhys hesitated. "They're twins, so maybe it's kind of like they dare each other to do their best. That's OK, but they need to lose the aggression now that they've proved themselves. They're top surfers – and they're awesome skaters as well. They'll be hard to beat in the skate comp next summer, that's for sure."

"And speaking of dares!" Toby looked straight at Rhys and laughed. "You lost the bet and when we get back to the city you've got to …"

"No way!" Rhys swallowed hard. "That stupid dare – I'd forgotten all about it."

"How convenient!" Toby teased him.

"What dare?" Brad looked blank. "What have I missed?"

"You don't want to know." Rhys winced and sank down into the chair. "Why did I make such a crazy bet?" He groaned again, wishing the dare had never been made.

"Rhys dared me to go in the comp." Toby was grinning broadly, totally enjoying the moment. "He promised that if I got first or second in my section, he'd join the all-boys tap class that I help teach on Friday afternoons after school. He taught me to surf – so I'm going to teach him to tap!"

"Fair enough!" Brad sprayed his mouthful of ice cream sundae across the table. "How old are the boys in the class, Toby?"

Toby didn't answer at first. He just kept on smiling.

"I didn't even think about that." Rhys suddenly felt really nervous. "I assumed they'd be my age. How old are they, Toby?"

"They're beginners, I told you – so they're five-to-eight-year-olds." Toby kept a serious look on his face for a couple more seconds. "Rhys should fit in really well, don't you reckon, Brad?"

In his rush to get away from Rhys, Toby almost knocked over his bowl of ice cream, as he jumped up swiftly from the table and raced to the safety of the bathroom, locking the door behind him.

"Thanks heaps." Rhys laughed, as he chased after Toby and banged on the bolted door."Great friend you turned out to be."

Then he recovered quickly, hoping he could salvage something out of the mess he'd gotten himself into.

"Hey, Brad, if Tobes is sleeping in there tonight, then we've got plenty of space out here. I think we should phone his sister and her friend – they might like to stay here instead of next door with the parents." Rhys rolled his eyes and strangled a laugh. "We can watch that video your dad took today – and we should probably get some drinks and stuff before the movie starts. Let's call room service again."

"Cool!" Brad put one hand over his mouth, as he unsuccessfully tried to stop the laughter and the ice cream escaping.

Rhys decided to sit it out. Knowing Toby, it

shouldn't take long. And sure enough, a couple of minutes later Rhys heard the bathroom door squeak open. He'd won. He was sitting with his back to the bathroom and with difficulty he resisted the temptation to look around. He wanted to seem totally cool.

"I assume the dare is off." He smiled confidently. "What do you reckon, Brad?"

Brad didn't answer. He just looked over the top of Rhys's head, indicating with a grin and a nod that Rhys should check out what was going on.

Toby was standing behind Rhys's chair, holding a pair of tiny tap shoes out in front of him, offering them to Rhys.

"Some people never learn, do they?" Toby's face was deadpan and he sounded like a teacher. "I thought we'd get a head start on your lessons this week – the parking lot is perfect for practicing. Nice and quiet! Here, try these – I won the Tap Championship in them when I was nine. I assume they'll fit. Or not!"

And, doubling over with hysterical laugher,

Toby ducked just in time to avoid the cushion that Rhys threw at him.

"Yeah, yeah! I get it!" And even though the joke was on him, Rhys joined in the laughter with his friends, as more cushions flew around the room. "As Dad always says: *He who assumes …*"

Acknowledgments

With special thanks for the generous support of the May Gibbs Children's Literature Trust which granted my fellowship at the Canberra studio in May 2004, making it possible for me to work on this project.

With thanks to my junior editors, my sons Damien and Henry Bell, and Alexandra Grylls; to my eldest son Ben Bell for the skateboarding detail, and to Phoebe Riggs for the surfing detail; to Courtney Dom for the cover art, and to Damien Bell for the chapter heading illustrations; and, as always, to my esteemed editor Gwenda who dares to care.